Paul Wilson has worked in a range of social care settings and is Vice Chairman of the British Association for Supported Employment. He is a winner of the Portico Prize for Literature for *Do White Whales Sing at the Edge of the World?* and his most recent novel, *The Visiting Angel*, was shortlisted for the 2011–12 Portico Fiction Prize. He lives in Lancashire.

MOUSE *and the* COSSACKS

PAUL WILSON

A complete catalogue record for this book can be obtained from the British Library on request

The characters and events in this book are fictitious. Any similarity to real persons, dead or alive, is coincidental and not intended by the author.

First published in 2013 by Tindal Street,
an imprint of Profile Books Ltd
3A Exmouth House
Pine Street
London EC1R 0JH
website: www.tindalstreet.co.uk

ISBN 978 1 90699 444 0
eISBN 978 1 90699 497 6

Designed and typeset by sue@lambledesign.demon.c.uk

Printed by Clays, Bungay, Suffolk

10 9 8 7 6 5 4 3 2 1

For Isaac, Lewi and Sam

1

THE FIRST THING YOU have to know about me is that I have no voice. I could shout at you but the space around us would be soundless. Sometimes I wish words would come out, but mostly I'm happy to be silent. It's safer that way.

My surname is de Bruin, which is fine. It's from my dad's side of the family, obviously. I think de Bruin is Dutch. I could tell you my first name, but I'm pretty sure you wouldn't like it. I know that because I don't like it either. Sometimes, when Mum gives me a hug, she calls me Mouse in a soft voice with her mouth cushioned next to my ear. *'Poor mouse,'* she says. So if I have to be called something, I'd rather it was Mouse, which seems to fit me just fine for the moment. My dad thought I chose not to talk. He said it was because I was a naturally unhappy child. He said I had a talent for it. I overheard him say to Mum, once, that I needed to pull myself together. But I'm not choosing. I really don't have a voice.

Sometimes I try to imagine what happens to all the words that get formed in people's heads but don't get spoken. I like to think of them floating up out of people. It would please me if that was what happened. They could drift away across the countryside. I think farm labourers in shirtsleeves could gather them up in the fields where the words had come to rest and bundle them together into sheaves of unsaid sentences, so none of them were wasted. They could be stored in cellars to stop them from drying out, or crumbling into dust. They could be kept safe there until they were ready to be taken into the city on the backs of carts and handed out to passers-by with clear voices, who would stand in market squares and in Sunday parks and patiently declare them so that, in the end, everything was said and nothing was left unfinished. If I were God, that's how I would arrange things. But I'm not God, I'm just Mouse.

2

I'M SITTING IN THE BACK SEAT of the car. I prefer to ride in the back. If I stretch out my legs my feet can touch the floor. Otherwise my legs sway to and fro as the car speeds up or slows down. I slide my glasses back up my nose and look out of the window. It's a long time since Mum drove the car. I try not to make it look like I'm paying attention to how she is doing. Her hands grip the wheel. Our belongings are piled on the back seat next to me. The city, where I've always lived, slips by outside.

It's the end of February and the afternoon light already looks grainy and tired. The lights showing in house windows are like lines of lanterns strung out for us as we drive past. They could be the lights of a festival we arrived too late for. I imagine people in the streets holding hands, dancing, but now the streets are quiet. Fields appear. The land ahead of us rises. The traffic slackens. The light fades. The road weaves upwards towards the moorland.

We drive through a small town in the hills. We pass a post box, a convenience store, a pub. Within a minute, the buildings give way to fields again. There's not enough light to see where they end. They melt away. Mum slows the car down. At a For Sale sign secured by a hedge at the side of the road, she signals left. We turn onto a dirt track that runs between two dry-stone walls. Mum drives cautiously over the ruts. At one point, she puts the handbrake on to check the directions again. She bites her lip, nudges the car forward once more. At the next low rise, the track swings left and a house comes into view ahead of us, beyond a huddle of trees. As we draw level with the house, we see a sign on the wall that says Bank Hey Farm (even though we know it's not really a farm). Mum turns into the yard. The front of the house is lit up by the brilliance of the headlights. She brings the car to a stop. With the engine still running, she closes her eyes in relief. One hand is still fixed to the wheel. I pretend not to notice.

It is clear, even from the outside, that the house is too big for us. In the last year we've lived in three different flats in the city, but Mum couldn't settle in any of them. She says this house is a bargain. It isn't expensive because it is *out of the way*, and because Mum signed a contract that says we will leave at a month's notice if, at any stage, the house is sold. Even though it is bigger and has land, it doesn't cost as much as any of the flats, but that isn't really why we're moving here.

'This is home for now, little Mouse,' Mum says.

I see that she has finally released her grip on the wheel. I nod and try to smile.

Mum takes out the keys the estate agent gave her and unlocks the side door leading into the kitchen. We edge inside, sniffing like mice at the damp. We wait to be startled, but the house stays silent. I reach out to touch the big table in the middle of the kitchen. I feel the grain of the wood. I wish we had wishes. I wish we were back in the city, but this is where Mum wants to be.

We carry our belongings into the house – four bags, two suitcases, my books and telescope, Mum's canvases, the quilts and pillows we squashed into the boot, Max's saxophone. We deposit everything in the stone-flagged kitchen. The total of what we have brought to start our new life takes up less space than the wooden table. Mum tries the light switch, then the tap. The pipe bangs. The tap gives a cough, then a pale brown water begins to hiss from it. While Mum watches over the tap to see if the water will run clear I go upstairs. The house smells of wet dog, of old milk. There is no shower in the bathroom.

Back in the kitchen Mum smiles hopefully at me. She fills the kettle with the clearer water now running from the tap. I open the kitchen door and stand on the step, looking out. There are stars in the sky – too many to count. The shapes of the hills sink into the gloom. As I look down the valley, the lights of Manchester are a luminous smudge where the dark land meets the dark sky. I read somewhere that when cities were bombed in the war, people in the blacked-out countryside could see the silent glow fifty miles away. I can't hear any sounds. There is no traffic noise, there are no sirens, no voices shouting. Maybe this is where someone with no voice is meant to live. Maybe that's how it works.

'It's chilly out there,' Mum says.

I close the door, but the cold continues to press in round its edges. Neither of us has taken our coats off yet.

Mum follows the instructions she's been left to fire up the range cooker, but it won't stay lit. There is a microwave. We eat soup and crusty bread at the big table. In the sitting room there is a wood-burning stove. We sit together on the sofa in the small pool of warmth, encircled by draughts. Thumbing through recipes in my cookbooks, I try to decide what to bake first in our new kitchen when the range is finally working.

'Are we okay, Mouse?' Mum says. She nuzzles my neck. We watch the unfamiliar shadows on the ceiling cast by the flames. I don't know what will happen next. I hope we don't have to be here long.

In bed I write, *Read me one of my old picture book stories.*

She rummages in one of the boxes of books. She reads me *The Tiger Who Came for Tea*. She knows it was one of my favourites when I was little. I imagine a tiger knocking at our big farm door, eating cake, drinking our taps dry, leaving politely, never coming back. I write a postcard. I go to sleep.

3

WHEN I WAKE UP the next morning, I notice a pair of men's shoes placed together in a corner of the room. They are brown brogues. The ends of the laces are tucked neatly beneath the tongues. An old man lived here for a long time. The shoes must have been his. It was dark last night; I was tired, and I didn't see them. I lift back the quilt and the cold air makes me gasp. I walk across the bedroom in my pyjamas and examine the shoes. I'm shivering. One wall is blank, as though furniture had stood there for a long time but has now been removed. The wall's emptiness makes it feel like a painter's large canvas. My opened suitcase is beside the bed. Hooked behind the door on a wire coat-hanger is a man's cardigan, abandoned like the shoes. It is almost as if someone else is still living here. But we know that the place has been empty since October. There is mould in the tray at the bottom of the fridge and the curtains in the sitting room are damp.

Last night, before I fell asleep, I lay in the darkness facing the blank wall, listening to the small sounds being made by the house, by the weather on its walls, by the wooden beams. Like sighs and breaths. Like the cracking of bones. They would have been the sounds the old man listened to in all the years he lived here, starting long before even Mum was born. They are his sounds, just like they are his shoes. This isn't our house.

Mum was warned that some of the man's possessions would still be in the house. His son has put the property up for sale and it was agreed with the estate agent to rent it out on a short-term lease until a buyer is found. The man's son, Mum said, agreed with the estate agent to move most of his father's belongings out of the way before we moved in.

In the light of the new morning we inspect the house. Mum rented it without coming to view the place first. She chose it from the photographs on the website, and from the estate agent's written description. We wander from room to room that way people do when they go on holiday, making little discoveries about light switches and cupboards. It becomes clear that the old man's son hasn't been very thorough in gathering together his father's things. As we move around the house we find reminders of this other life that was lived here. A jam jar crammed with pens, a scarf on one of the coat hooks in the hallway. We discover a file under a bed with invoices and receipts, a shoe box at the back of a wardrobe shelf with a handful of photographs and an old army ID card inside. One of the photographs is of a boy, about my age, standing on a beach. The photograph is black and white, slightly out of focus. On the back, someone has written: *William at Southport, 1933*. Behind a curtain on the windowsill in my bedroom where I have set up my telescope is an open book, face down, seemingly left at the last page it was read at. The author's name on the front cover is Isaac Babel. Beneath the dressing table's mirror is a slim, wide drawer. I try it, but the drawer is locked. Downstairs on the kitchen wall, a telephone number – someone's mobile – has been left chalked in big blue numbers on the white plaster. The back room overlooking the walled garden has been converted into a study. The shelves inside are still lined with books. In the outhouse, among stacks of plant pots and seed trays, are half a dozen plastic boxes in which, it seems, many of the man's belongings have been stored.

Mum puts Max's saxophone, on its stand, in the hall for want of anywhere better to store it for now. She sets up the easel and her stock of canvases in the bay window of the sitting room. She's a good artist, although it's not her job. She likes painting trees. I always liked to watch her paint when we went on holiday. Her trees were wonderful. Long rows of pale beech trees. Lines of silver birches. Firs. Winter trees. I suppose she paints the trees now from memory, but somehow they are just as beautiful, as if she can still see them by simply looking hard enough into the blank of the canvas stretched on the easel.

Back in my bedroom, I look at the photograph I took from the shoe box. In the photograph the old man who lived here is a boy. Short trousers. Bony knees. Pale face. Does he know the camera is pointing at him? Perhaps he prefers to look away at the long stretch of sand, and the sea. The beach looks too big for him. He is the only figure in the picture. I look at his shoes again. I try his old man's cardigan on. It comes to my knees.

4

'LAST NIGHT,' MUM SAYS, 'when we went to bed, I think you must have ended up with the old man's bedroom. We can swap if you like – if it bothers you. Or you can have the box room if it feels cosier in there.'

I think about it.

What was the man called who lived here? I write out on a page from my notebook.

'Crosby?' she speculates. 'Something like that. William Crosby.'

I think about the boy on the beach. I think about the William in the photograph, whose old man's shoes wait for him in my room.

Each time we move house (we have moved four times now in the last year if you count the first move from our house on the avenue), we seem to have fewer things to take with us. It feels like pieces of our lives are disappearing bit by bit. As a result, we only seem to inhabit a small part of the farmhouse. Our things are outnumbered by those of the man who lived here before us. It feels like William Crosby is still the stronger presence here.

The fruit loaf I made sits cooling on the kitchen table, denser and darker than it should be. Mum says it looks fine. She is making soup. She seems happy to be here now she has managed to fire up the range, preparing soup for the two of us in the old man's kitchen. The act of making soup is, I have come to learn, one of her safe places. If I wake up during the night and go to the kitchen for a glass of water I will sometimes find her quietly making soup.

'It's all right, Mouse,' she will say. 'I couldn't sleep. That's all.'

I know what it is. It's the owls. I know she hears them and that they keep her awake.

'Are you okay for now in that bedroom?' she says.

My telescope fits on the windowsill in there, I write, as if this is a real answer.

I put on my coat. As I fasten the zip, I feel the weight of the Filofax on one side. I put my hand inside the other pocket. I feel the edges of the postcard I wrote last night.

The coat is an old padded anorak of Mum's. It's the one I nearly always wear. Mum says it's too big for me. She says I could get lost in it, but I like to wear it because the pockets are just big enough to fit the Filofax in even as it grows fatter, and because, in the end, Mum gave up fighting me over it because there were 'bigger fish to fry'. I like that it's a squeeze to fit the Filofax in the pocket of my coat. That way, there is less chance of it falling out somewhere or getting stolen when I'm out walking. Also, the coat has a deep inside pocket as a safe place to keep the phone that Mum bought me last year for my tenth birthday.

My Filofax has a dark red leather cover. Mum calls it wine-coloured. It is divided at the front into sections. On each of the dividers are the headings I printed out for the four sections I use:

Things I Can't Do
Things I Shouldn't Do
Things I Don't Know
Things I Got Wrong

I keep the book with me all the time. It's important, because whenever I think of something I can write it down. That way nothing gets forgotten. It isn't that I'm stupid. It's just that there are a lot of things I still need to know. I worry that I won't remember them if I don't keep a list:

Swimming a length
Travelling in time
Choosing a new name

The good thing about using a Filofax is that it has ring-binders, so I can keep on inserting new pages. That way, I won't ever need to start again with a new book, and the lists in my four sections can keep on growing. The pencil slides neatly into a space down the spine, and the book itself fits with a gentle push in the pocket of my coat. I open it up and flick through the pages to find the next blank sheet. At the top I print: WILLIAM CROSBY.

I go outside. A dusting of snow has fallen in the night. The cold stings my cheeks. I watch my winter breaths unfurl in the air in front of me. I can hear crows barking to announce themselves up in the trees. The wood-store leaning against the side of the outhouse is three-quarters full of logs split down into pieces for the wood-burning stove. The old man's logs. The old man's stove.

The path leads round into a walled garden at the rear of the house. The walls that shelter it from the winds make it feel like a secret place. There is a bench with its back to the house looking out onto the garden. Down the sides of the three walls that shelter the garden are raised beds. The space in the middle has the remains of last year's crop of vegetables decaying in the snow among its stakes and canes and lines of wire mesh. On the ground, chickweed and moss have taken hold. In a far corner are two clumps of rhubarb with their first curled shoots showing bravely above the ground. I sit down and pull out the postcard from my pocket. I read what I wrote on it last night.

Max, Is it possible ever to have time go backwards? I would

like to have something changed that has already happened. I just need to know. Love, Mouse.

I walk around the narrow path that circles the vegetable plot. The door in the far wall opens onto a scruffy patch of ground that the online description of the house called a paddock. I stand at the edge of it looking round. My eyes trace a line over the trees, then across a white field that begins level then drops away to a hedge in the valley. After that, the land rises up into a drift of other people's fields touched with snow. I'm not used to all this space in one go. The sound of the breeze rises and falls. It's like the land breathing.

The rental agreement Mum signed says we have two acres with the house. I set off to trace out our boundaries. As I walk across the paddock, a pair of crows on the ground watches me crossly as though it's me who is trespassing and not them. I run at them. They beat their wings and take to the safety of the branches. I walk across to the copse where the crows have settled. They watch me. One of them squawks in protest, but they don't feel the need to move further away. I choose the tree furthest from the house. On the side facing down into the valley, I pin the postcard to its trunk with a drawing pin. I don't wait around or anything afterwards. I don't wait for Max to turn up. I don't *pray*. When it's done, I just move away.

I walk back across the paddock and pass through a gate into the bigger field. The winter grass where it perches above the snow is the colour of straw. The ground is pockmarked with tufts of reed. There is a hand-painted notice fixed to our gate that the old man must have put there. PRIVATE. NO ENTRY. BEWARE OF THE GUARD DOG. I walk on. Halfway down the slope I realize there is someone watching me. A figure is standing at the edge of the field. Our field. The old man's field. He looks like a man, but he stands there like a boy, with a boy's low fringe. His weight is pressed to the gate. His arms are draped over the top bar, as if he is waiting for something. In the space between me and him a scattering of crows is dotted about the field. I stretch out my arms and make a run at them down the hill. The birds take to the air, vexed, complaining. And the man, as if he too is another crow for shooing, turns and flees.

Catch a tennis ball
Leave a trail
How birds know where to fly

I sit on the dressing-table stool in my room, looking up through the telescope at Venus. It's easy to find Venus because it's the brightest thing in the night sky after the Moon. It's the same size as the Earth, but we couldn't live there because its atmospheric pressure is nearly a hundred times more than it is here. I told Mum about the atmospheric pressure on Venus. I think it comforts her that I can remember stuff like that. I think it helps her to worry a bit less about my not speaking. I turn to face the bedroom. I realize I know quite a lot more about Venus than I do about the man who used to live here. I go to stand in front of the blank white canvas of a wall that faces my bed. There is a pattern of holes in the plaster where screws once held the furniture in place. Now it's an empty wall, anticipating the first something to begin filling it again. I pick up the photograph of William on the beach at Southport and hold it up to the wall. I find a drawing pin and fix the photograph in place. I sit on my bed, looking at William, aged eleven, surrounded by the empty, waiting wall.

5

THEY SHOT THE HORSES one by one. What else was there to do? A bullet in the head of each of them, tethered, as if this was a reasonable way to bring things to a close. As if horses, all along, had been the enemy. They fell like dynamited buildings fall, as though they had never been animate. Only on the ground did their limbs thrash with something close to memory. Their tongues rolled. The echo of each pull of the trigger rebounded off the sides of mountains and came back to us like mockery. Three hundred of them, too sick to give to farmers, too weary to wander off into the hills to forage for themselves in the way that two thousand others did. Bang. Bang. Bang.

Local people, oblivious to the trenches of blood they waded in, hacked them up in the fields where they had fallen and carted pieces off in wheelbarrows to eat, while those of us in uniform looked on, pretending we were distanced from it. It was a morning's work. It was the final act.

6

Go to school
Texting people I don't know
Listening for owls

I WAS SIX WHEN MY VOICE started to disappear. I was eleven last week. I don't think anything happened to make me stop speaking. It just happened. It gradually faded, then one day it vanished. Like a clock stopping. It's not such a big problem for me. I text a lot.

It's like being at the cinema. You're expected not to talk at the cinema. If you do, people hush you. I used to go to the cinema a lot with my friend Lucas. His mum would take us. We got shushed sometimes when Lucas was talking. I didn't mind him talking because I prefer books to films, but I used to go because Lucas liked to watch the films *and* talk at the same time, and because he made me laugh. I ought to say that there isn't any noise that comes out when I laugh. It happens silently, like everything else, but we still got shushed because of the noise Lucas was making. That's because you're meant to go to the cinema to watch what happens and to listen to the actors. People *pay* to keep quiet and watch the film.

Lucas has been my best friend for quite a long time. I know that because I know all the things that make him happy, like going to the cinema, or reading about Leonardo da Vinci, or taking machinery apart and putting it back together again. I know that when he was nine he worked out how to fix his mum's lawnmower when it broke. I also know the things that make Lucas sad, like sudden loud noises, and the fact that Leonardo da Vinci never got to build the helicopter he designed.

I don't go to the cinema any more. Lucas thinks I live in London now. That's what I told him. I didn't want him knowing that we still lived quite close to Manchester. It's better that way. These days Lucas and I just text. We don't get shushed for that. Instead of going to the cinema, I like to walk a lot. That way I can watch people, and listen to them, and it doesn't cost anything.

Stop marmalade cake burning at the edges
Cry like other people

If I need to tell somebody something, or ask them a question, I write it down on a blank sheet torn from the back of my Filofax and show it to them. Sometimes they write the answer for me on the same page, as if I can't hear them. People are funny. Sometimes I write down for them:

My ears are fine. It's just my voice that doesn't work.

It's true that there are some things that are harder when you have no voice. You can't shout for a dog if you're taking him for a walk and he runs off. That happened to me. That's why we didn't get another dog. There are other problems as well with not having a voice. You can't sing. You can't go 'Ouch!' if you trap your finger. You can't tell your mum stuff. Not some stuff, anyway. Sometimes, when we curl up together on the sofa, I can make a tiny noise come out. But when I want to say things I have to write it out for Mum like I do for everyone else, and there are some things that are quite hard to write down.

I'm undertaking a research project about how happy people are. I understand about research. I got a telescope for my sixth birthday, and the more powerful one that I have now when I was nine. I like reading about what it is that scientists think is out there in space, and how the scientists keep finding out new things so that what we think is out there keeps changing.

The thing about having no voice is that you can research things quite well because you're mostly on the outside looking in. It gives you the chance to watch people and listen to them. You can hear the things people say because the sound of your own voice doesn't get in the way. I use a scale from one to ten with decimal points as well, so I can get the levels accurate and detect even the smallest changes. I watch people and score how happy or unhappy they are. It's a very scientific approach. I'm recording my findings at the back of the Filofax

My own average is 4.6. It goes down if I get worried about things, like whether Mum is eating enough, and why I'm quite skinny but not in a good way, and it goes up if I'm doing something interesting like reading or using my telescope, but it doesn't ever go higher than 5.2. My average is obviously higher than Mum's, who, is at 3.1 at the moment, which is okay for her, although her scores get lower when the owls keep her awake. I think my average is lower than most people's. It's especially lower than the scores for Sadie, who I go to once a week in the city for speech (ha ha!) therapy, who averages 8.4. I can't imagine being an 8.4. I think Sadie must really like her job.

It was Max who told me about the owls. At breakfast one time I asked him if he had heard the noises that had woken me up in the night.

'You mean the owls?' he said, reading the question I had written out for him.

I nodded that I understood, not wanting to seem stupid. For weeks after that, I found myself thinking about the owls. I pictured them as grey and serious, with large yellow eyes and almost human faces, swooping into our house at night through windows we must have left open. The flapping of their wings was surely as faint as whispers. They perched, I supposed, on the tops of cupboards and the backs of chairs. Then there was another night when the same cries woke me. Max must have heard them too because, a few moments later, he crept into my room and sat next to me on my bed. I reached for a pencil.

I don't think they were owls this time, I wrote on a piece of paper.

He looked at my note curiously. Then I think he realized what I meant. He slipped his hand in mine.

'Not owls,' he whispered. '*Yowls*. The *yowls*. The shouting.'

Only then did I understand that what we had both heard wasn't the sound of an animal at all, but the sound of muffled arguments downstairs, the cries of anger from a woman holding back somewhere in her throat in a vain attempt to avoid waking her sleeping children upstairs.

I heard the noises twice more in the weeks that followed, but although I recognized them now as human shouts and cries, I found that I still instinctively thought of them as owls. After that, whenever Mum couldn't sleep, or the onions for the soup made her cry a bit, I would think to myself that the owls must have returned. Although I couldn't hear them, I knew the sound of the owls must be there inside her head.

Play the piano
Fall in love

While we are setting up the computer and printer in the study someone knocks at the door. It startles us both. We're not expecting anyone. Mum goes to answer it. I look at the rows of books lining the shelves, reading the names of the authors and the titles. On the bottom shelf I find an ancient portable typewriter. I lift it up onto the desk. When Mum returns, I've cleared the desk of everything except the jam jar full of pens and I've lifted the typewriter up onto it. I look at her to see who was at the door.

'It was a man asking for someone called Irena,' she says.

'He thought someone called Irena lived here.'

I shrug.

Mum nods. 'I told him an old man used to live here. I don't think I convinced him. His English wasn't very good. He gave me a card with a number on. He said if she comes back I should ask her to ring the number he gave me. I took the card just so he would go away.'

She smiles at me to show me everything is okay. I know she doesn't like unexpected things like that happening.

I run my fingers along the keys of the typewriter.

Do you think it works? I write, partly to distract her from worrying about the man at the door, and partly because the typewriter does look interesting and I've never seen how one works before.

Mum takes the piece of paper with my question written on it and winds it into the typewriter. She taps out 'qwerty'. The arms flick forward and the characters snap against the paper. The carriage jigs sideways. The letters appear faintly on the paper.

'It needs a new ribbon,' she says. She points to where the keys bang against the thread of ribbon from one spool to another. She goes back to setting up the printer and fiddling with the broadband box. I resume working my way along the shelves, inspecting the lines of books that belonged to the old man. I remember that I need to start reading the book written by Isaac Babel, which the old man left in the bedroom.

'Do you want us to find a local library near here?' Mum says from below the desk. She finishes connecting the line to the socket and rises to her feet. She reads the note that is waiting for her on the desk.

I think I'll read some of the books in the house first.

7

HAVING NO VOICE MEANS I have a lot of time for reading. I have a list of books I've already read, and a list of the ones I want to read soon. I keep my lists in the Filofax. When we moved into our first flat I went searching for the nearest library. Mum knew it was important to me, so she agreed to come with me because I needed an adult to alter my details on the computer and get a replacement card. We made the journey in a taxi. The new card they gave me, like the one it replaced for the library I'd used before, looked like a credit card with my details on one side next to the Council's badge, and a barcode on the other for the library computers to scan. Obviously, the first thing I did when we got back to the flat was to scratch out my name with the edge of my door key, just like I'd done to remove our surname on the name card next to our buzzer at the front door of our block.

The deal I made with Mum in return for her going with me to the library was to agree to start secondary school when the next school year began. Mum said she had to tell the education officer *something*. It was all very well saying that she was home educating me, she said, but we didn't really have much to show the woman, did we? I suppose she had a point. Even though I'm supposed to write reports on some of the books that I read, and even though I'm meant to choose topics to carry out research on, I don't always show them to Mum, and when I do she doesn't always get round to marking them. It's not that she's not clever – she is. It's just that she gets distracted by those other fish she has to fry. So in the end I said she could tell the education officer that I would start school when the next academic year began, partly because September was far enough away not to feel real, but mostly because I needed her help to get the new library card.

Mum says when I go back to school I'll need a new name. She says I can't go answering to 'Mouse' all my life. I suppose she's right, but that's still a long way off. There are a lot of pages to fill before then. A lot of books to read. A lot of things I need to learn.

Keep soufflés from collapsing
Draw trees

I carry Max's saxophone out to the outhouse, which is where Mum and I have agreed it should go for now. I stand it in the corner, away from the storage crates, which I have worked out must have been packed by William's son. I arrange the crates out on the floor, so I can look for any more interesting books to read that might have been left in them by accident. Taped to the lid of each crate is a description of its contents: CROCKERY, PANS, HAND TOOLS & POWER TOOLS, ORNAMENTS & PICTURES, CHARITY SHOP. BATHROOM. None of them says, BOOKS. I look inside some to check their contents. Inside the Bathroom box are two of William's razors and a pair of spectacles, but also some women's toiletries and a hairbrush. I'm not sure why these are here because he lived in this house on his own.

Down one side of the outhouse is a row of gardening tools hung on a series of hooks and nails. Under the window is a workbench built from heavy wooden planks. There are three cardboard boxes on the workbench – the kind that supermarkets leave out for people to pack their groceries in. On each of them is written CONTENTS FOR BURNING in red marker pen, in less certain handwriting than the block capital labels on the crates. I open up the first box.

It is full of words. There are slews of paper – foolscap, envelopes, lined notepaper, the backs of letters or bills on which words have been typed. Single words, words connected into phrases, linked together into sentences. Sometimes a line of words is repeated on a sheet of paper several times, as if someone needed to see the phrase typed out over and over, or as if there was some kind of code which the person slamming the same keys again and again was trying to crack.

Every now and then there is a sheet of paper on which the words become descriptions of people or events, or reports. There are unfinished letters already addressed to people. There are descriptions that end suddenly halfway through a sentence. Reading random lines from pages here and there, I notice that whenever the letter 'c' has been typed out it lies slightly sunken and tilted on its axis to the left. Each new 'c' always seems on the verge of falling backwards, as though it might eventually tip over all the way onto its back and become a 'u'.

Inside the other two cardboard boxes are notebooks, newspaper cuttings, letters, but also more sheets of paper with phrases or sentences typed on them. I lift out handfuls of the paper and sift through them, glancing at words that catch my eye, at sentences. I stop at a sheet that has a single typed phrase repeated line after line all the way to the bottom of the page. It says:

Who out there has uncovered me?

Underneath the workbench is a stack of identical cardboard boxes that have been flattened. I lift one out onto the bench. When I flip it over, I see that the same three words – CONTENTS FOR BURNING – have been written on the side of the box in red marker pen. Each of the other boxes, when I pull them out, has the same thing written on it.

I go outside. In a corner of the yard is an oil drum raised off the ground by a set of bricks. A piece of corrugated metal serves as a lid for the drum. I lever the lid off and let it fall to the ground. At the bottom of the drum is a layer of damp ash together with the buckled binders of several notebooks or journals – the kind that Mum used when she was making notes about cases she was working on. I picture William standing here, dropping words into the drum, watching the flames catch the paper. I don't know whether doing it made him happier or sadder. How do you score someone who sets fire to the words he has written? I picture him standing on the beach at eleven, the boy with all those words coiled inside of him, waiting to emerge. They could have been important. Or useful. Or just beautiful. And, anyway, there must be lots of people like me around the world (even though I've not met any of them yet), who have no voice. If they're like me, they'll get through an awful lot of reading. They need all the words they can find to read, and there are only so many libraries, so many books. One day, they might run out. I feel sure that whatever pages were set on fire in the oil drum should have been preserved.

Back in the study, I turn the roller on William's typewriter, so that a clean piece of the paper is showing, and then punch each of the keys in turn along the bottom row of letters. The 'c' tilts to the left. It is printed slightly lower than the characters on either side. I sit at the desk, imagining William sitting here, typing, looking out at his walled garden. In the photograph in my bedroom he is still eleven, his eye drawn not to the camera but to the sea. I want to know how much of an eleven-year-old is still part of someone who is very old. Are they the same person? If you could somehow bring the boy to life, would he recognize the old man that he has become? Or would he pass him by on the street, not knowing that this was him? Would I do this to the old woman who is me? Will I look back at scrawny Mouse de Bruin at the end of my life and wonder who she was and where she went? If, by then, my own words have returned, will I remember how it was to be a Mouse with no voice?

I pull open the three desk drawers in turn. The first one is empty. The middle drawer has a single piece of paper in it. It's a letter addressed to William. It was sent to his house. To our house. Its one sentence says,

> 'We are instructed by the Singer family to return all the enclosed communications as the hotel is closing down, and we regret that no further assistance can be offered.'

It is signed by a man called Emile. The address he wrote from sounds German. He was returning something to William, a lot of things – papers, perhaps, documents, letters – but I don't know what they were about, or whether William saved them, or burned them.

I open the bottom drawer. Inside is a batch of typewritten letters. They have the tilted 'c' from William's typewriter. Some of them have pencilled crossings-out and new words inserted between the lines, but they are all set out with addresses in the top right-hand corner, as if when they were typed the author imagined they might be ready, or nearly ready, to send. Most of them have William or William Crosby typed at the bottom, with a space above his name for a signature. One of them is signed off 'Dad'. It begins, 'Dear Rebecca.' It has corrections running throughout its four pages. One whole paragraph is crossed out, and 'not right' has been written in pencil in an imaginary margin down the side.

I take a handful of the letters upstairs to my room. I choose a place on the far side of the pale wall from the photograph of the young William, and pin up the letter to 'Rebecca'. I stand back and look at the space on the wall between the boy and the letter to his daughter. Beneath the letter, I catch sight of the pair of shoes placed neatly together in the corner. I walk over, take off my own shoes and step into them. I look down at my feet in William's shoes. I shuffle to the centre of the room in them. In the photograph taken on the beach, he looks solemnly out as a child towards the sea. He is the only figure in the picture. I pin up some more of the letters. They look small against the wideness of the empty wall. I smell his cardigan. I can smell his smell.

◆ ◆ ◆

'Are you sure?' Mum says as I climb into bed. She is holding the book I've passed to her to start reading to me. I nod my head. It's William's book; the one I found on the windowsill, the one by Isaac Babel.

I love Mum reading to me at night before I go to sleep. She reads beautifully, as if there is no hurry, as if she understands everything, as if all of it matters. She reads a chapter or two a night, depending on the book. When she reads to me, she forgets the outside world. I can hear it in her voice.

'It's a complicated book,' she says. 'Short stories. Will you tell me if you lose interest?'

I nod in response. I can feel the blossoming warmth beneath the cover. I am safe from the cold that crouches beyond the quilt and brushes my face.

Mum opens the book, steadies herself and begins to read.

'Although our little town is not large, although its inhabitants are few, although Shloyme has lived for sixty years in the town without a break, even so, not everyone would be able to tell you who Shloyme is, or what he is like. That is because he has simply been forgotten, in the way that an unheeded, inconspicuous object is forgotten.'

I lie curled into the quilt, listening to Mum reading to me from the book that, not so long ago, William was reading in this room.

8

The year before

OVERCOATED AGAINST THE Pennine cold, hands jammed into pockets as if he might be trussed for slaughter, William Crosby sits upright on the bench he had constructed as a young man in his first summer here. One or two of the houses across the valley have lights cast against their windows. The sky above him, after the long night, is still soft and unresolved.

He can recognize the narrowing of his life. A corner of a room, a place by the window, a strip of floor, as Rilke had observed. No more journeys into Manchester, not so many down into the town. No great desire; no love of crowds or cities. There is a family-run Italian restaurant that he goes to once a week, a convenience store for milk and groceries, an occasional poker game that runs on Thursday evenings at the kitchen table of a retired engineer called Maurice. William turns up when the mood takes him. There are three others who play. They are men who are happy to stay on the surface of things, to let the cards talk. There has always been a reserve about William, even as a boy. He could stand outside of things. It was never a need of his to become known.

The breeze around him slackens and falls away. In the pause, he thinks he feels the year's first promise of warmth from the March sun. Here is one final spring. Another chance to calculate whether a life lived so long can hold some meaning. In a life of steadfastness, one last cause to take up. And, abruptly, for no reason he can immediately pin down, he pictures the boy waving to him from down among the avenue of cypresses at the Villa San Lorenzo, and he is overwhelmed.

The first time he set eyes on the farm was on a June day. There was a blue sky overhead. There was meadowsweet in the ditches. William had been hiking for hours. He took his rucksack off and sat with his back against a dry-stone wall looking at the place, and decided there and then that the house would be his.

It wasn't a working farm, although a farm was what they called it from the start. It was a farmhouse, partially roofed, virtually abandoned, damp sunk into its thick walls when he and Margaret bought it, and just enough land – a steep-sided field and a space for horses or goats – to be called a smallholding. The house was half a mile along a track from one of the minor roads that climbed out of the Manchester conurbation past Saddleworth Moor on its plodding route over the spine of England to Yorkshire. William remembered that the air was filled with birdsong that first day, although he couldn't see any birds. They were in the grasses, or down the valley, their calls rising up the hillside on warm air, but he was already imagining the place slowed with the heaviness of winter, the moors dressed with snow, ice lacerating the gulleys. He was picturing the land bleached clean and remote.

There was no For Sale sign anywhere, but it was clear no one had lived there since the war. It was 1951. He had started teaching as a way of funding the writing that he hoped would come. They had a little money in the savings bank from Margaret's share of the sale of her family's terraced house. The shelter her parents had been in had taken a direct hit during an air raid on Manchester. Now William was her family.

He agreed to have children in return for her acceptance that they should buy the farm. He had been firm until then that he didn't want a family. The deal was as perfunctory as that. Margaret was in love with him. He knew that. He supposed a jury might say he played on it. She wanted the domesticity, the comfort of family duties, to take her mind off any flickering doubts that William was any different to the would-be poet with the dark eyes who had proposed to her. That was on his last home leave before the war took him away for two and a half years. He simply couldn't be any different. He was her life.

It took him a month of enquiries to find out to whom the house and its scraps of land belonged.

9

Visit Lucas
If there are 350 billion galaxies, whether there's another Mouse somewhere where things happen differently to me

IT BOTHERED ME A LOT that things weren't always what they seemed. When I started showing an interest in baking, Mum taught me how to make ginger parkin. But I wanted to learn more than the single recipe Mum knew by heart, so she bought me a recipe book, and I borrowed some more from the library. The cakes in the photographs looked delicious. I would read the recipes all week, making notes, and then on Saturday mornings, while my dad was with Max at orchestra practice, or swimming, or cross-country, I would spend the morning baking, with Mum on hand while she did her background reading for the following week's cases, as general dogsbody for me – retrieving ingredients from kitchen cupboards, adding items to my never-ending shopping list, supervising my use of the oven.

Mum says I'm a perfectionist. But it seems to me that it was Max who was a perfectionist. It was just hidden because he didn't need to try very hard. I'm told that the first time Max picked up the saxophone he could blow a note on it. His embouchure (that's the proper name for how your mouth fits around the reed) was perfect. At least, that was my dad's version of what happened. I know that when Max let Lucas have a go, the noise he made sounded like a small animal in pain. As for me, I couldn't get any sound at all to come out. The saxophone and I were enemies from the start. It was the same for me with gymnastics, netball, rounders – the list of practical things I can't do is pretty long. I can put together an impressive list of things that have defeated me. I always sensed that, if there was *something* I could find a talent for, I would stick at it. I think that's why I read a lot.

I quite liked baking from the first time Mum set me to work standing on a stool creaming soft butter and brown sugar together in a bowl. So it began to bother me that, whenever I baked something, the finished product didn't always look like it did in the photograph in the recipe book. My version would have caught on the side of the tin, or become stuck to the baking parchment, or wouldn't have risen evenly, or would be still slightly gooey in the middle.

'No, honestly, it's good,' my dad would say when he and Max arrived home.

'It's *really* good,' Max would say, usually reaching for a second slice.

It's not even level, I would write. *It looks like the Leaning Sponge of Pisa.*

Mum said I shouldn't worry about things looking perfect. 'You're doing great,' she said.

But my cakes never look like they do in the book, I wrote.

'Those photographs aren't real,' Mum said. 'They use all sorts of tricks to make the food look delicious on the page, but you wouldn't want to eat it after everything they've done to it to make it fit to be photographed.'

You mean it's fake? I wrote.

'It has to be,' Mum said. 'The food would dry up under the hot lights of a studio and wouldn't look very appetizing. So they spruce it up for the camera – make it *look* perfect.'

I think I must have looked a bit crestfallen that my new-found passion for baking was based, it seemed, on a sleight of hand.

'Give yourself a break, little Mouse,' Mum told me.

I told Lucas about the fake food.

It's not real, I wrote. *Can you believe it?*

Lucas was nonplussed. 'They do it in films,' he said. ' An actor gets ready for a fall, or a car chase, and then they cut so that the stunt man can take his place to do the dangerous stuff and just make it seem like it was the star who raced the car over the cliff, or drove the speedboat through the jetty.'

It all seemed a long way from the simplicity of Max blowing clear notes out of his saxophone. It made it hard to know when you were being told the truth, and when you were just being fooled by a set of circumstances dressed up to *look* like the truth.

I have decided to find out more about William Crosby – the man whose house we are living in. Whichever room you walk in, he is still there. The pieces of his life are all around us. It wouldn't feel so surprising if, each day, it were his footprints being freshly laid, if his book on the dressing table was resting a few pages further on each time I checked. Meantime, it feels like Mum and I are just passing through. If we vanished tomorrow, people would hardly know we had lived here, just like they would hardly have known we had stayed in each of the three flats in the city that we rented. A girl who makes no sounds, and a woman who lives indoors, painting trees that aren't there on to canvases that no one will get to see.

I know what Mum is doing; she is trying to keep me safe. She sticks to the same safe routines for us both – the making of soup, the eating of meals, the painting of trees. It's a world that seems to get smaller as it repeats and repeats. No wonder she is starting to forget other things – how to make anything except soup; how to go outside; how to be a barrister. Her pale complexion is paler still, as though even the bit of colour she once had is disappearing. My dad reckoned that when she was younger she spent too much time indoors studying. Perhaps this is how it will be from now on, with the two of us becoming less substantial each time we move somewhere new. Perhaps, in the end, we'll simply vanish into thin air. Perhaps that's how ghosts are made.

On each of the next two mornings, the man-boy with the funny haircut reappears at the bottom of our field. I don't run at him any more. He stands and watches me. I try not to catch his eye. I don't make any sort of gesture as I pass him. He says nothing to me, and that makes me nervous. I walk the length of the hawthorn hedge and turn back up the field towards the house. When I glance back over my shoulder at the gate, I see that he has turned and gone. I decide to find out where he goes. I walk back to the gate. From there, I can see the bob of his head above the wall as he walks away along the track. I set off in pursuit.

Where the farm track meets the road by the For Sale sign, the man turns right, heading down the hill towards the village. I have a better view of him now. His arms move stiffly, as though his torso is hinged a bit too tightly. He doesn't hurry. He doesn't look back. I follow him, twenty paces behind until he gets out a key to let himself into a house halfway along a small terrace. I make a note in my Filofax of the address. Later in the day, I sit at the computer and type:

> Dear Sir or Madam,
>
> I am concerned about the man who comes and stands at the edge of our field each day. He is not doing any harm but he doesn't say anything and it is a bit worrying for my daughter. Also I am not sure if he is lost or if there is a problem.

The reply comes back two days later in the post. It's a letter signed by a woman called Mary.

'Dear Ms de Bruin,' it starts. 'I'm very sorry if you and your daughter have been upset by Anthony.'

I am surprised by how much the woman has written to me. Her letter is four pages long. Of course, she couldn't know that the person who wrote to her is only eleven. She thought I was an adult, but, even so, it seems like a long letter for her to write to a person she has never met. I suppose that she wanted to explain about her son in the same way that I hear Mum explaining to people about me – even though I'm eleven and he is a grown man. Perhaps she was bothered by the thought that her son had unnerved us. There *is* something odd about him, so I suppose she might be used to talking about him. Maybe it gets hard, having to keep explaining the same things to different people. Sometimes, I can hear Mum's voice get a bit weary when she's having to tell someone again that, even though I don't have a voice, I can understand everything perfectly well. Mum says the same things over and over to people, but they don't always seem to understand. Maybe they don't believe her. Perhaps, like my dad, they think I should just pull myself together. Maybe, when people ask the woman about her son, she finds herself telling people more and more about him. Maybe she hopes that, in the end, she will say enough for someone finally to understand what she is telling them.

I tried to work out what would need to change in order for my own scores to rise. Sometimes small things help: when a cake comes nicely out of the oven; when the night sky is clear enough of cloud for me to use the telescope; when I find a good place to leave a new postcard for Max. I left one this week on a tree I found at the edge of our land. It said, *Max, I'm sorry I didn't cry at your funeral. Yours sincerely, Mouse.*

I made some notes at the back of the Filofax while I was working out what kinds of things might help raise my scores. The first idea I had was for there to be a rota for people to be quiet. One thing you realize when you have no voice yourself is that everyone else speaks too much. They talk all the time. There's no one listening out there. And every so often, I thought, maybe once a month, there should be a day when no one says anything while they're outside, so that everyone moves quietly about in the streets and on buses and trains for the entire day. They would smile, and use sign language, and ping texts to each other silently, but no one would say anything.

I also made a note that it would help if there were signs when you were walking around the city like those KEEP OFF THE GRASS signs, but these signs would tell you things you could do, things that would make you happier if you did them. The signs could be on the sides of buildings or by the side of the road. They could say THROWING STONES IN THE WATER IS FINE or THIS IS A FRIENDLY PARK, COME IN AND SIT ON A BENCH AND NO ONE WILL BOTHER YOU.

And I thought it would be helpful if people wore a badge that displayed their current happiness score. The badge would work like a thermometer, but instead of measuring someone's temperature it would register how happy or unhappy the person was. That way, you'd be sure to know how to act around them without them having to tell you, or without you getting it wrong.

Finally, I wrote that there ought to be safe spaces every so often along the pavements and paths where people walk. They could be painted on the ground as white circles. If you stepped inside one, you had to be left alone, like the rule about being out of reach in a den when kids are playing tig. That way, when you were going somewhere and you didn't want people to bother you, you could be sure of arriving safely by moving swiftly from one circle to another.

I've begun to think of Mum getting through each of her days like this. She moves carefully from safe place to safe place. For a time, she didn't move *anywhere*. She would sit in the flat, not looking like she was doing anything.

Are you okay, Mum? I'd write, and she would look surprised and read the note and smile and say she was, but I knew she wasn't. In the end, just like she buried Max, I think she buried some of the things that threatened to overwhelm her. Now she can at least get around from safe place to safe place, from small task to small task, as long as she can keep remembering where each of those pieces has been buried. After all, if she forgets where one of them has been hidden away, it could go off under her foot like a small grenade.

10

My dearest girl,

I have seen heaven. It is a real place. The sky there is a blue so polished that it dazzles the eye. In the mornings, before the day's warmth starts to unfurl, there is a dew in the fields, and in the stillness of that first hour steam rises from the flanks of horses.

I have been there – I have walked amidst it all – and I write so that that you will know a little of it too, so that you will come to believe in the possibility of such a place. Its appearance is that of an enormous valley surrounded by high, snow-topped mountains and carpeted with green meadows. It is a gathering of all the generations. Weary people who have seen their courage tested greet each other respectfully as strangers, or rekindle old friendships. Impossibly old men with deep lines and long beards mingle with young boys skittering about the place. Mothers carry babies. Families break bread together. Couples walk hand in hand. Soldiers in archaic uniforms and widows in black feel the kiss of the sun on their faces. After all, surely those who have been through the trials of Hercules are entitled to some small respite. This is, as heaven must surely be, a final place of safety, a sanctuary.

Their number is too big to count. This valley is an impossible size to comprehend, stretching so much further than the eye can see. And for people to move about the place (for even in heaven people must carry out daily chores to see to their own quiet welfare and that of their loved ones), there is every conceivable kind of transport from centuries past through to the modern technological era. Men ride on horseback without saddles as they did three thousand years ago; harnessed horses pull carts and gypsy caravans; precarious bicycles are ridden unsteadily along tracks by the river; motorbikes and cars – jalopies and sleeker modern designs – pick their way patiently between pedestrians along the single road that runs through the valley and allows for commerce and communication between so many people gathered together in one place.

I can tell that already your imagination is failing you. Your intuition is causing you to doubt the ramblings of a deranged man you have never met, despite my claims to know who you are. I can only beg of you to persevere – to take a leap of faith and imagine that such a place exists, that it is populated by people who, if they met us there, would embrace each of us with joy. And, as if to test you further, I will say that this place I am describing to you gives out the perfect warmth of a May day, and that every Sunday the bells of the churches sound across the valley, and people gather together in the open air to give thanks and celebrate ancient services of prayer.

It was my habit while I was there to pass through the valley each day. One woman I met there turned round from the field in which she was exercising her horses and, in her rudimentary English, shouted across to me, 'This is heaven, yes?'

'Yes,' I confirmed for her. 'This is heaven.'

'I'm not see heaven on the map,' she said.

'No,' I agreed, laughing. 'Not on the map.'

'What is called on the map, please?' she asked me.

She meant the maps of statesmen and soldiers. She was no more than passingly curious about the place she found herself in under that impossibly polished blue sky. The name itself had no real significance for her, and so I told her.

'Drau valley,' I said, and she nodded, happy to have it confirmed that the place she found herself in was a reality to others and wasn't something that she, and only she, had dreamed.

11

Max's favourite colour
Algebra
Riding in the front seat

AS I'M RIDING ON THE METRO going into Manchester, I get a text. I feel the *ping ping* through the lining in my coat. The buildings we glide past in the tram are getting bigger. The grandest ones were built when the city was important because of the cotton industry, when the Town Hall and its clock tower had to be substantial enough to feel like the very centre of England.

Mum said that, even though we've moved out of the city, I should resume seeing Sadie for my weekly speech (ha ha!) therapy. Mum offered to come into Manchester with me if I wanted her to. I told her I was fine on my own. We agreed that it was enough for her to drive me to the Metro station in Bury, which is as far as the line goes out north of the city, and that I would ride in from there on my own. That way, I could practise my independence, which would please Sadie, and Mum could practise two short drives once a week.

'Text me when you get there,' she said when we had bought my ticket from the machine, 'and then when you've finished with Sadie.'

I might look in the shops for a bit, afterwards, I wrote down for her.

'Okay,' she said. 'Remember to tell me when you're heading

back to the tram so I can be waiting here to pick you up.'

I look at the text message that came through on the tram. It says, *Who is this.*

I get texts all the time. But, apart from Lucas, the only ones that come from someone I know are from Mum when she texts me to say, *WHERE ARE YOU* or *COME HOME FOR TEA I MADE SOUP.*

I tried to persuade Mum to text me without writing everything in capitals. At first she claimed that she couldn't remember how, but then she said she preferred sending me texts in capitals. She worries when I'm out. She wants to know where I am. She thinks texting in capitals is a way for her to speak louder, so I'll hear her and not forget to reply straight away. If I don't respond fast enough, she sends me the same message a second time. When that happens, I sometimes reply by texting, *I KNOW, I KNOW.*

Apart from the texts from Lucas and Mum, the other ones I get are mostly from people who are replying to me. The response I get most often is, *Who is this.* The other one I get a lot is, *Why are you telling me this.* I think they ought to put question marks at the end of their questions, even when they're texting, but most people don't. If they respond, I always try to explain why I sent them a text. Sometimes, someone will reply again, usually with another question, but mostly that's all that happens.

The most replies I've managed so far from someone I don't know is a five-text conversation before the person stopped. I have a rule, though, never to send a message to someone if there's been no response to my previous text because I know that when Mum does that with me it can be a bit irritating, which means I never find out why people stop texting me.

Last week I got a text from Lucas that said, *What should I do about your present?*

He'd remembered that it was my birthday. Every year since Lucas's family moved into the house two doors down from us on the avenue, when he was six, he has remembered my birthday and bought me a present. I always liked how his gifts were wrapped in too many sheets of wrapping paper, and how he always presented me with them very solemnly. Sometimes I think that Lucas is more comfortable taking lawnmowers apart and reading about Leonardo da Vinci than he is spending time with people. He doesn't have Max's winning smile. He would stand blinking at someone, then suddenly say something unexpected like, 'Did you know that Leonardo da Vinci wrote everything backwards?', which I thought was quite interesting, but which other people sometimes thought was a bit odd.

I knew for certain that if I texted Lucas back to say there was no way I could arrange to see him, he would just ask for my new address so he could send my present through the post. I didn't want to refuse point blank to give him our address because that would make him suspicious. But I couldn't make up an address in London because then he'd post the present down there and it would come back marked as 'Address Unknown' because he's so organized he'll have written 'If undelivered please return to Lucas Greaves at…' and then his own address on the back of the parcel. I could have given him an address in London and then arranged to have it posted back to me in Manchester, but the trouble is I don't know anyone who lives in London. I could have asked Sadie if she knows any speech therapists in London, but then she might have wondered why I was asking and she's already quite interested in Lucas and how he's doing and whether I've seen him lately, because obviously I haven't told her that Lucas thinks we live in London now. Each time Sadie asks about him, I have to try to remember what I told her the last time because she remembers what I tell her really well.

In the end, I told Lucas he couldn't post my present to me as we'd had to move out of the house in London that Mum's firm had put us up in because it had an infestation of basking flies in the attic, and so the house needed fumigating. I told him the man from Environmental Health had told us that gable-end houses are prone to basking flies, which like to congregate on the warm end wall. Then, to distract him from asking for the address of the hotel, I texted, *Me and Mum are getting the early train from London on Thursday. We are in Manchester for a few hours, she has someone to see about work, then we're going back. If we can meet at 2 at Piccadilly Gardens you can give me my present then. Okay?*

I get off at the Metro stop in Piccadilly Gardens but, instead of heading straight to Sadie's office as I usually do, I walk a slow circuit all around the edge of the square. I need to be sure of a good vantage point from where I can look out for Lucas when I've finished my session with Sadie. And Lucas *will* come, because I know he wants to see me and we haven't met in nearly a year – not since Max died.

While I'm sat in reception on the ground floor of Sadie's building waiting for her to come down and collect me, I take out the letter I received in the post from the man-boy's mother that I've brought to show Sadie.

A text comes in from Mum. *WHERE ARE YOU*, it says. *IS THERE A PROBLEM.*

No problem, I reply. *Forgot to say I got here safely. Sorry.*

I can't remember why I started to text people that I didn't know. I think the first time was when I was emptying numbers from my phone memory, not that there were a whole lot to start with. I decided to keep Lucas's number, but I got rid of the others. I did it by deleting the numbers one digit at a time. I knew I could just have hit a button to wipe out the whole number in one go but doing it bit by bit made it feel more definite. It helped me to feel sure that each of the numbers had gone for good.

Of course, a lot of the numbers I deleted weren't the names of people but of places, so the captions for the numbers said things like School, or Doctor, or Library. When I got to the last number in the phone's memory (apart from Mum's and

Lucas's, which I'd left on), I deleted the final digit first. It was a seven. But then, instead of deleting the next digit, I typed in an eight to replace the seven. I looked at the new number I had created by changing just the final digit. I sat there for a while wondering who owned this new number, and how far a text would have to travel to reach him or her. I typed in, *Is anybody out there?* and pressed the send button. A day later I got a text back saying, *Who is this.*

After that, whenever I felt like texting (especially if I was still waiting for Lucas to reply to the last one I'd sent him), I would create a new number by changing the final digit and use it to send out something I wanted to say in a text. The morning after we arrived at the farmhouse I made up my latest new number, but I haven't had a response as yet to the message I sent it. This usually means that the person has deleted it, or that it's not a number currently in use. In my experience of texting people I haven't ever met, which I explained one time to Sadie, if there's been no reply after three days then it's likely there isn't going to be one at all.

Sadie told me that, a long time ago, they used pigeons to transport messages written on tiny rolls of paper strapped to their legs that could be sent over hundreds of miles. So now, whenever I send a text to someone I don't know, I like to imagine it as a bird being released from my hands to carry my message away over the horizon to whoever is going to receive it. Sometimes I get a reply, sometimes not. I know Mum doesn't like me doing it. She thinks it might annoy people. Sometimes the message I send is, *Is anybody out there?* Other times, I text about something I've read that day that I think is really interesting or important. *Scientists say we only use 5% of our brains, isn't that great.* Sometimes I ask questions. *Do you think birds know that they're singing?*

The text I sent to the new number I made up three days ago said, *How many things that people wish for in a life do you suppose come true?*

◆ ◆ ◆

When I sit down in Sadie's office she asks me how my week has been. She always starts like that. She likes to know what I've been up to. She calls it a warm-up for the speech (ha ha!) therapy, but sometimes she gets so engrossed in what I've been doing that she forgets to get round to the real speech therapy until near the end of the session. I like Sadie's office. It's very bright and clean. I sit next to the whiteboard on a swivel chair so I can write my responses for her on there, rather than keep using pieces of paper from my Filofax.

'That way,' Sadie says, 'we're saving a nice-sized forest each week.'

Sometimes, when I'm thinking of how to answer a question Sadie has asked me, it's good to go round slowly in a full circle in the chair until my thought is properly formed in my head. It's important to give myself plenty of thinking time because I have to be careful not to break any of Sadie's Three Golden Rules which are 'deal-breakers'.

1. Tell the Truth.

2. Always Get Permission from the Other Person before Breaking off from a Session.

3. Respect Each Other.

I also have to be careful because I think it's possible that Sadie isn't completely what she seems.

She asks me if our old house on the avenue is still for sale. I write down that it is. I tell her what our new house is like. I write down that it's far too big for us, and quite cold. She asks if there are any good points about it. I write on the board that it's a good place to use my telescope because there's not much light pollution up there and I can see a lot more in the night sky there than I could down in the city. She asks me about light pollution, so I write down how it's easier to see planets and stars and asteroids when the night around you is very dark and not too spoiled with artificial light. I know Sadie is more interested in people than in science, so I stop then and tell her a bit about William Crosby – about the old man's belongings being left in the house. She asks me if he was a farmer before he got old and had to move out. I write down that there isn't enough land for it to be called a farm. I tell her that I know William was in the army. I tell her I think it's possible he might have been a spy. I explain about the man-boy standing at the edge of our field, and about the letter I received from his mother. I show her the letter. I watch her carefully as she reads it. Sadie has a long face a bit like a horse, and big feet. She wears sandals. When I wrote this down the first time we met (Sadie said I had to describe her) she laughed. She said what else, so I wrote, *You dress like a jumble sale,* and she laughed some more. What else? she said. I wrote, *You smile very nicely.*

'I hoped we'd get to a compliment in the end,' she said.

While she is reading the letter, I write down on the whiteboard, *What is a pluck?*

Sadie looks up. 'It's the internal organs of an animal,' she says. 'A sheep, usually, I think. Its heart and liver and lungs.'

I pull a face.

She frowns as she tries to put together the pieces of the story contained in the letter from the man-boy's mother. 'So the old man who lived in your house before you – he thought the woman's son had killed his cat?'

I nod in confirmation.

'And he was so angry about it that he went down into the town and nailed the pluck to their front door?'

Another nod.

'But, in fact, her son had just been returning the cat's body to him, so he could bury it?'

I point to the part in the letter about the group of boys from the town who tease the woman's son all the time. Her letter says it was one of them who shot the cat with an air rifle.

'Do you think it sounds like her son might have a learning disability?' Sadie says.

I write a question mark on the whiteboard.

'Learning disability? Hmm. Well, it means it takes him longer to learn how to do things. He might have to be taught how to do things in a different way to you. It's possible, for example, he might not be able to read and write.'

He looks old but he acts like a boy, I write on the board.

Sadie nods. 'Maybe he thought the man would want to bury his cat. Maybe that's why he took it back to William's farm.'

He doesn't speak. When he stands there he doesn't do anything, I write down.

'Do you do anything?' Sadie asks.

He's a grown-up, I write in protest.

12

I TOLD LUCAS TO MEET ME by the Queen Victoria statue in Piccadilly Gardens. I remember sending out a question once when I was texting that said, *Why do you think they called it Piccadilly Gardens when it isn't a garden?* When the person who received my text finally replied, they said, *Who is this.*

Why meet there? Lucas texted back. *We could meet in the Caffè Nero in the middle of the square. I like the muffins they sell there.*

Wait at the fountains, I told him. *I might not feel like going to Caffè Nero.*

This was a lie, but I thought, all things considered, it was okay to tell it.

I always like going to the coffee house in the square. For one thing, it's true that the muffins are really good, especially the lemon poppy seed ones. For another, Pavel, who often serves me when I go in on a Thursday after my session with Sadie, is always nice to me. Even when I went in the first time and handed him my order on a piece of paper instead of saying it out loud, he didn't act as if I was a crazy person or an idiot. He didn't say anything smart or clever about it. So, when I was leaving, I put ten pence in the tips box. Sadie is always saying I need to do one good thing for someone each day. Not for Mum, she says. That doesn't count. Everyone should do good things for their mum. With me it's mostly baking. But if I'm going to do a good thing for someone else, a different person each day, then Sadie knows I have to go outside, and not just to the library. She says that this way she knows I'm getting in some practice at being around people for when I go back to school.

The first time I put my ten pence change in the coffee cup on the counter they use for tips, Pavel wrote 'DZIĘKUJEMY' on my receipt, which I think was a good thing to do.

I can hear just fine, I wrote down for him.

He read the note and then made a short bow from behind the counter and said 'Dziękujemy!', which he does every week now when I put my ten pence change in the cup.

I approach the spot on the edge of Piccadilly Gardens from where I have worked out that I will get the best view of Lucas arriving sometime in the next half hour without being seen. But when I get to my position, I can see that he is already there.

Although I write to Lucas and we text each other several times every day, I've not actually seen him for eleven months, but I know straight away that it's him, even though he has his back to me, and despite the fact that he's definitely got taller in the meantime, unlike me. I don't think I've grown at all in the last year since I last saw Lucas. Not in any way, because I've been checking for any sign of breasts and there's definitely nothing there. I told Mum and she said not to worry as they'd come along any day now. That's easy for her to say, but I just smiled when she said it because she was being kind and she doesn't want me to worry. I look at my watch. It's only just past one thirty. Lucas is sitting on the steps beneath the statue of Queen Victoria, who dressed in black all her life because she loved her husband who died when he wasn't very old. I text Lucas to check it really is him.

How you doing?

A minute later I get his response. *Got here early. You in Manchester?*

No, I text back. *We're on the train. It's running late.*

I wait for the reply. *I'm fine,* it says, *don't worry, I brought a book.*

I make a note to score Lucas as 6.2.

◆ ◆ ◆

Sadie says that relearning to speak is like acting – like learning to play a role. I told her that it was so long ago when my voice started to disappear that I think my insides have forgotten *how* to make the sounds. She says when someone in my position is relearning how to speak, it sometimes helps if they start off by imagining they are someone else. They think of themselves as playing a role in the same way that an actor does on a stage. That way, she says, it's not so scary, which means their insides might be able to remember what to do.

When she said that, I wrote on the whiteboard, *There's someone else in my position?*

When I told Mum what Sadie had said about acting, she said that being a barrister was a bit like that. In court, she said, you had to be something of an actor. Of course, you needed to analyse all the evidence and put your case together, she said; you needed to understand the law (which is why she spent so much time inside reading law books and staying pale); but unless you could stand up and command the court, like an actor does in front of an audience, you weren't very likely to win for your client. We were living in our second flat when she said that. I suggested that maybe Mum could try acting when she needed to leave the flat. She could pretend to be someone else. Once she'd done that, I said, maybe she would be able to pretend to be a barrister again for a while. But she hasn't tried it yet. The best she's done so far is to pretend to be someone who can drive. She says it's fine, that the office sends her work to do on cases so she can keep her hand in until she decides to go back. I'm not so sure. I don't see her working.

Sadie has suggested that, when I'm ready to begin practising talking out loud, I can start by being on my own, just pretending there is someone in the room with me. She asked me today who I might want to do my pretending *to*. I said I didn't know. She asked me again later on in the session when we'd just been laughing about something silly. Usually, I'm good at keeping my concentration in the sessions with Sadie, remembering not to say things I shouldn't, but something made me write down Max's name on the whiteboard.

'Not Lucas?' she said, sort of casually.

I was remembering Sadie's Three Golden Rules. I shook my head. *I can just text Lucas,* I wrote.

'Would it be easier to pretend Max is in the room with you because he's dead?' she said.

Sadie can be like that, sometimes. She just says things out loud that people wouldn't normally say.

I nodded.

'Maybe that's what we'll do, then, some time,' she said.

I shrugged.

'You could be an actor playing a part, and you could pretend as you're doing it that Max is sitting in the room with you. D'you think?' Then she just moved casually on and started talking about something else.

I have a pretty good view of Lucas round the corner of a shop window. He is hunched over as if he has settled down over his book. Now and then he slides his glasses back up the bridge of his nose. At any given moment there are always a few people passing between us or just standing there talking on their phones, so it's unlikely he would catch sight of me even if he looked across in my direction.

I send him a message. *Announcement on the tannoy says there's a problem delaying the train.*

What about your present? he replies.

Ask for Pavel in the Caffè Nero, I tell him. *He will look after it. Tell him it's for Mouse. Me and Mum will walk down there when we get in to Piccadilly.*

I'll wait for a while, he says. *Maybe they will fix the train.*

I go back to watching him. Every now and then, I see him raise his head to look vaguely around the square. I wait another fifteen minutes. I text to say the train has come to a stop, and the train manager says we've broken down. *You should go,* I text, *just leave my present with Pavel.*

In the end, it's nearly half past three before Lucas concedes defeat. He stands up and walks across the square towards the Caffè Nero. As he does so, I can see his new elongated shape clearly for the first time and it surprises me a bit, but then I remember that when I last saw Lucas it was at Max's funeral. When he emerges from the café a few minutes later, I can tell from the way he is walking, not looking round at things any more, that he is not as happy as he was when he arrived. I mark him down in my book as 4.8. I feel bad for him, but I know I have no choice. I wait until he is out of sight, then let another three minutes pass just to be sure the coast is clear, then I go across to Caffè Nero myself.

Pavel hands me the package that Lucas left with him. He's very nice about it, but I can see he doesn't really understand.

'I'm not telling him you come here every week,' Pavel says, 'Just once or two times from London. That's right?'

I nod.

'He seems a nice boy. You don't want to see him, no?'

I shake my head. I give him a thumbs-up to say thank you for the parcel, but on my way out I forget to put anything in the tips cup.

I'm already sitting in my seat on the stationary tram before I remember to text Mum so she can drive down to meet me at the Metro's terminus. I unwrap the present Lucas left for me with Pavel. It's a new Filofax, a blue one. Inside the front cover, there's a note from Lucas asking me to send him an address so he can write me what he calls 'real letters' instead of just texting. Behind the note, written on the flyleaf, he has written, *A new notebook for a new start.* I want to tell him that I don't need a new notebook, that the one I've got is fine. Even so, at the top of the flyleaf I write, *Mouse de Bruin, Bank Hey Farm.*

As the tram sets off I watch people walking across the square carrying their bags and holdalls. I think about the sheep's pluck I told Sadie about, the one that William carried through the town and nailed to the man-boy's front door. How did he get it to the house? Did he hold it over his shoulder in a bag, or drag it through the town along the ground? Did it leave a trail smeared on the pavement? As it hung on the front door of the house where the man-boy lives with his mother, heart at the top, then lungs and finally liver, did it drop spots of blood onto the doorstep? I keep thinking about the sound of the big nail being banged with a hammer hard enough into the door to hold its weight.

The man-boy's mother said in her letter that she was alone in the house when the pluck was nailed up, and I keep wondering what she was feeling as William was hammering his nail into her front door, and what she thought when the noise stopped and she dared to open her door and found the organs of the animal and the drops of blood on her doorstep.

She told me in her letter that the day after she had written to William, telling him what had really happened to the cat, a package was pushed through her letterbox. When she opened it there was money inside. She counted it up. There was nine hundred and eighty pounds. She said she knew it was from William. She knew she couldn't accept it. She had known William Crosby, she said, a long time ago when she was a girl.

I put Lucas's Filofax on the seat next to me and lift out my own from my coat pocket. I flick through the pages until I come to the one that says WILLIAM CROSBY. I have already written down seven pieces of information. I add a number eight and write next to it: 'Nailed a sheep's pluck (heart, liver and lungs) to a front door.'

As the tram draws slowly out of the city, I feel a text come through. The message isn't from Lucas, or from Mum. I look at the number illuminated on the screen. The number ends in 266. It's the new number I made up earlier in the week, the one I sent a text to three days ago that said, *How many things that people wish for in a life do you suppose come true?*

The response from 266 doesn't say, *Who is this* or, *Why did you send me this.*

It says, *Do you think that, one day, someone should write the history of wishing?*

I feel pleased that the person who replied has remembered to put a question mark at the end of their text.

13

EVEN BEYOND EIGHTY, he has discovered, the confirmation that death is at hand is a rebuke. *So you thought I had forgotten you?* Death seems to say with a coy smile. *Out of all the countless millions, some small infantile part of you really imagined you might escape me? You thought it possible that you could keep going unnoticed. Another week, another month, on and on?*

Immortality by stealth. But no one escapes, although the truth of it has taken him by surprise. Until now, all he has ever known is life.

The only person who knows is the consultant who told him. Maybe the lab technician who tested the biopsy? Maybe someone who typed the information into the computer? How long does he have left? Who knows? Not the consultant, that's for sure, equivocating away in a drawl measured out to be as neutral as water.

'It's never easy to say at the best of times, Mr Cosby,' he had said, as he contemplated the painting on the wall over William's left shoulder. 'And there's the additional factor of your age.'

'Oh, for Christ's sake, how long?'

The consultant had switched his gaze to look out of his office window. 'A few months. Six. It really is hard to say. Look, is there anyone you want us to talk to? Family perhaps? Children?'

'I want you to talk to me. *Talk* to me.'

'We'll be able to control the pain if that's troubling you.

The meds are very good in that way these days. The advances have been remarkable. You shouldn't have any fears on that score.'

'I'm lucky, then? It could be worse? Things could be worse?'

'I'm not saying that.' The consultant swung his gaze back inside the room. It passed surreptitiously over his watch and settled again on the painting. There was a pause. The sound both men could hear was the steady effort of William breathing in and out, the crude imitation of a young man's casually drawn breaths.

'When Isfahan revolted against the taxes being imposed by Timur Beg,' William said, 'Beg ordered the complete massacre of the city. When it was done there were twenty-eight towers, each of them constructed out of fifteen hundred heads.'

'You are a student of history?'

'I was a teacher. I taught for forty years. I read history for my degree, and now I'm going to be history.'

The consultant adjusted his position.

'Basilius the Byzantine emperor…' William began.

'Mr Cosby, can I…'

'*Basilius*, the Byzantine emperor, blinded fifteen thousand Bulgars. His soldiers left one in every hundred men with one good eye to lead the conquered army home. Can you imagine the logistics of an operation like that? Do you suppose they queued? In Italy I saw a shell hit the next fox hole to mine. The man in it had a helmet that he boiled his clothes in to wash them. The boiling had turned the helmet black. The colour of his helmet was the only way they could identify who had been hit.'

'You fought in the war?'

'Body parts across Europe and I came out without a scratch.'

'You have a lot to be grateful for. Is that what you're saying?'

'Well, I'm not a defeated Bulgar, for one. And I'm still here. I'd have settled for that on the slopes of Monte Cassino. Wouldn't you? Have settled for that? Sixty more years. *Of course* it could be worse. There isn't anything you can think of in this world that couldn't in some form or other be worse. Jesus *Christ*.'

The consultant straightened a cuff. 'So what is it, and I hesitate to ask this given the inevitable upset of the news you've been given, do you think that makes you angry with me? The anger is understandable, necessary even, but your energies will need to turn soon to the support you may need to manage your situation.'

William had raised himself up to his feet – a gradual process these days – and rested his weight on his cane. 'My name is *Crosby*. William *Crosby*. Now if you'll excuse me, I have a life to finish living.'

14

Talking to dead people
Hold my breath for one minute
Stop plum cake sinking in the middle

IS TALKING TO DEAD PEOPLE wrong? Obviously, in my case, I don't actually *talk* to Max, but I write down what I want to say on postcards and leave the messages for him in places that he liked. I know he liked trees.

Talking to a dead person is different to praying. I know praying is *like* talking (even though it's usually done silently in your head), but praying is when who you're talking to is God or Jesus or one of the saints. People usually pray when they're asking for something – for peace in the Middle East or for somebody to recover from cancer, or when they want to say sorry for doing something wrong. But you don't ask dead people for peace in the Middle East, not if the dead person you're talking to is your brother.

I went to church for a while after we moved into the first flat. I stumbled across it when I was out finding my way around our new neighbourhood. I didn't realize until I went inside that it was a Catholic church. I'm not really sure what the differences are between the various churches. The advantage of finding a Catholic church near our flat was that the priest said a Mass every morning. I asked Mum if she minded me going. She said no, but I think she might have meant yes. I think it would have been hard for her to say yes. Maybe she thought that at least it gave me a good reason to go out of the flat. Maybe she thought I was just planning to go to the church on Sundays. Sometimes in a morning she'd say, 'Are you sure you want to go *again*?' I think Mum wished that whatever it was I was praying for when I said my prayers in the church I was saying to her instead.

'We should talk more, little Mouse,' she says sometimes.

That's okay, I write on the next blank sheet in my Filofax. *What should we talk about?* But sometimes it's hard to talk when only one of you has a voice.

I stopped going to church after Lucas texted me one morning during Mass. When my mobile pinged, the priest stopped what he was doing on the altar and glared at me until I went red.

The only person who knows that I talk to Max is Lucas. I asked him in one of my texts if *he* talked to him, too. Lucas replied that when Max was alive it was mostly Max who did the talking and me and Lucas who listened, so it would feel odd now, Lucas said, if *he* was the one doing the talking. And it was true, when I think about it, that when the three of us were together it was mostly Max's voice people would have heard. Lucas didn't seem to mind. In quite a lot of ways, he was more like me than Max was.

Lucas is a year older than me, and very nearly a year younger than Max, although they were in the same class at school. When I first met him he was kicking a ball about in the avenue with Max, although I could tell his heart wasn't really in it. He liked watching things, he couldn't run very fast and, like me, he was happier listening rather than talking. He must have been happy for Max to do most of the talking, because he was always coming round to our house to play with both of us. He didn't mind that I was a girl. He didn't even seem to mind that I had no voice. He says he can remember when I could still speak, although my words were already starting to become faint. I'm not sure I believe him, because even I can't remember what my voice was like. Anyway, he always remembers when it's my birthday.

I don't think Mum would be happy if I told her I was talking to Max. Mum is an atheist. When I asked her why, she said that barristers were trained to look at the evidence, and to build their arguments on the facts at their disposal. She said she was pretty sure there was no compelling evidence for God. Mum thinks that death is the end of things; that Max isn't still out there, in heaven or anywhere else. If she knew about the messages for him that I leave pinned to the trunks of trees she might say that I was wasting my time because he wouldn't be able to see them. She thinks there isn't a Max any more. I don't know what my dad thinks. If I asked him, he would most likely say it's hard enough dealing with the problems that *living* people cause without having to worry about whether or not to say anything to dead ones.

Dear Lucas,

You asked me for my address so that you could send letters back to me instead of just texting me. That will be nice when we can do it, but it isn't possible just yet and here's why. We've still got a problem with the infestation of basking flies in the house we were meant to be moving into. We've had to relocate temporarily into a hotel that Mum's chambers are paying for. We might only be here for a few days as we don't know yet how quickly the fumigation will work and we can't go back there until all the flies are gone. I will let you know how this is going. Meantime, the hotel we're in is interesting and very nice. As you know, this is my first time in London. The doormen at the front of our hotel wear heavy overcoats with gold braid. When you walk in they raise their hats. The lobby you walk in to is white and art deco (which is a style from the 1930s) and it has a big central staircase that curves upwards, but hardly anyone goes up and down it because they all take the lifts. The towels in our bathroom are super thick and fluffy. We get fresh flowers in the room each day, which I like. We have a view of the London skyline from our balcony. We can see the River Thames, which runs past below. Also St Paul's and some other things. The people staying in our hotel are certainly an interesting group of people. The women are very beautiful and glamorous and the men wear suits. Most of them wear sunglasses. I haven't seen anyone famous yet, but I'll keep a watch-out. Mum and I dress for dinner and we have our own table by a potted palm tree on the roof terrace. When it's fine, an orchestra plays there after dinner. Last night I stayed up a while and watched the couples dance while boats drifted past on the Thames below us and above our heads the stars were sparkling in the sky. It was delightful. I'll text tomorrow night to make sure you got this letter. Mum says Hi.

Love,
Mouse

Sadie says, 'Your mum told me that she left your dad once before – that you and her moved to another house. Do you remember that?'

I'm not quite sure where this is going. It may be the kind of apparently harmless question Mum would once have asked in court, having first dug a great big elephant trap for the witness in the road up ahead. Wherever we're heading, I feel the need to correct Sadie.

And Max, I write on the board.

'Sorry?' she says.

Mum and me ***and Max*** *moved,* I write.

'Yes, yes, sorry,' she says, as if she forgot, which I doubt. 'Of course it was, it was the three of you. So how old were you then?'

Seven, I write, *and Max was nine.*

Even though I don't particularly like talking about Max to anyone, not even Sadie, I don't like it when it feels like he is being forgotten. I don't like it that he is fading away. Sometimes I think that's one reason why I started calling into the church for early morning Mass when we were in our first flat. The other reason was that it was a good way to put some structure into my day. Sadie likes me to report on the structure of my day. The church was also somewhere no one expected me to say anything. But mostly going to Mass was a way of trying to stop Max from disappearing completely. I didn't want him to be gone for ever. I don't write that down for Sadie on the whiteboard.

'But you all moved back?' she says. 'To the house on the avenue, with your dad?'

I wait for her to speak again, because she already knows that's what we did.

'Was that your mum's idea? For you all to go back and live with your dad.'

I nod.

'But you didn't mind, you and Max?'

Can we do speech therapy now? I write.

'Can I ask one more thing?' Sadie says.

I shrug.

'Why do you suppose your mum chose to move back to the house with your dad?'

Because she loved him, I write.

Mum said that we had to go to the community centre. We sat in the back of the taxi while the man drove us there. She asked me how I was feeling. I didn't write anything down. I looked out of the car window. It was nine weeks after Max's funeral. We had a new flat with a narrow balcony. If you stood on it, you could hear the children's voices from the playground of the primary school at the end of the road.

'Just be nice,' Mum said softly. 'Just do this for me. Okay?'

In the community centre, we went into a big room. Mum

said we should sit down. Two women came in and started talking to us. They smiled a lot. One of them asked me how I was doing. She said I could take my coat off if I wanted. I shook my head. Mum stood up and said she'd just be in the room next door. I took out my Filofax and wrote down, *Can we go home, please?*

'Your dad really wants to see you,' one of the women said. 'He just wants to say hello. To ask how you're doing. That's all.'

I watched Mum and one of the women go out of the door we had come in through. The other woman walked across the room to a different door. She opened it, and then I could hear her and my dad talking in the corridor beyond the door. I closed my eyes. I drew my knees up under my chin. I wrapped my arms over the top of my head so that my head was tucked down tight into my chest. I made myself into a ball. I was as small as I could make myself. I wondered what it would be like to become invisible. I wondered what you had to do to make yourself disappear completely. I kept my eyes closed. I *felt* invisible. It was dark and quiet down where I was. There were voices around me, but somehow they seemed to be a long way away. I don't know how long I stayed like that. Eventually, I heard Mum's voice whispering in my ear.

'Little Mouse. Come on, little Mouse.'

There was only Mum in the room. The two women had gone. My dad had gone. I think Mum had been crying.

In the study I type out an email to the estate agent using the address on the letter they sent to Mum confirming the rental agreement for the house.

> Dear Mr Taylor,
>
> As you know, we are renting Bank Hey Farm. We have found some unposted letters that might need sending to family

and friends. If William Crosby's son, who is renting us the house, has an email address can we have it so we can ask him what he wants us to do with them.

Yours respectfully,
Ms de Bruin

It seems pretty clear to me that the study is still William's room, not mine and Mum's. He sat at this desk every day for more years than Mum has been alive. Also, the letters he drafted to people in his last months here are still in the bottom drawer, waiting to be sent. I come in here when I want to think. I sit in the armchair, one fingertip cushioned nicely into the old cigarette burn in the fabric of the arm. Or I sit at the desk looking out of the window onto the garden protected by its three walls of slate – in the same way, I suppose, that William did each day of his life.

I read through what I've written on the computer screen, then press 'send'. It's quiet in the house. I expect Mum is painting. Or dreaming of painting. Behind me, one of the books on William's overcrowded bookcases tips softly from its shelf. It lands with a slap on the floor. The sudden noise jolts me.

15

THE SUDDEN NOISE JOLTS HIM. The motion jerks the bowl William has been cradling in the study. The handkerchief tucked into the collar of his shirt catches some of the soup, but splashes drop onto his trousers and on the cushion of the armchair. In his momentary fluster he isn't sure what the noise signifies. He looks down at the stain on his crotch. He tries to wipe the stain with the dry edge of the handkerchief, but he succeeds only in rubbing the soup into broader smears against the pastel of the corduroy. It occurs to him finally that someone is knocking at the front door. He stays quite still in his chair. The door to the study is pushed closed and the blinds are drawn. The banging resumes. It is more insistent this time. He feels a swell of anxiety in his stomach. It rides up inside him and settles inside his ribcage. He has an absurd, momentary urge to cry as if he were a boy again. It subsides. He reaches for the button on the radio and turns the music off. It was chamber music. He can't remember who by. He wonders if he dozed off while he was eating. It happens sometimes. He holds the now almost empty bowl of soup in his two hands on his lap, trapped and hesitant, waiting for the knocking to cease.

At one point during the winter, William had taken to his bed. He was putting his coat on to go down into the town for porridge and washing-up liquid, and perhaps a newspaper, and he decided instead to go to bed where he stayed for a week, maybe two – it was hard to tell. He had a Scotch when he woke and one when he could see that the sun was going down, and in between he lay perfectly contented beneath the sheets. If he felt hungry he nibbled cheese from the packet, or Bourbon creams until the tin was empty. The hours, inconsequential as high cloud, passed over him. He was serene. He thought of himself as jettisoned, like an astronaut in space watching the lunar module drifting away. He felt the steady tug of the earth moving on its axis through each day without him.

It was the discomfort he gradually started to feel that drove him out of bed to the health centre in the town. It was the doctor's requirement for tests and the appointments they necessitated that galvanized him into a routine. It was the casual death sentence at the hands of the consultant that gave him a new clarity. He began to prepare letters; for his son, his daughter, former colleagues, neighbours, people he'd known half a lifetime, others he had never met, for people he believed may still be alive and those he knew for sure were dead. The drafts piled up on his desk. In the middle of the night he would riffle them, searching for the one that was going round in his head, sometimes expanding what had to be said, the next night editing fiercely, leaving each of them bruised and shapeless, and himself pale, dark-eyed and briefly satiated. He woke in his armchair in the study one night to find one of the drafts gripped tightly in his fist and the stub of a cigarette in the other hand pressed into the indent it had burned in the arm of the chair.

Each time he settled to write, driven by this new zeal he felt, he was compelled to recognize his failings, the extent to which his life had fallen short, the people he had disappointed. There was satisfaction in judging himself so harshly. It was a liberation, like stepping out of his own skin. When each new notion opened up inside him, he grabbed for paper and a pen in case the thought dissolved into the air before he could fix it to the page. Things needed to be said. He felt consumed by the need to round things off. He wanted nothing unresolved.

The single bang that comes next has a different quality to

it. It is denser. It is the sound of something solid striking the front door and meeting the resistance of the catch. There are two more hefty strikes, followed by the crack of the casing splintering and the noise of the door as it swings open and hits the wall with a clatter. Then a hesitation.

'Mr Crosby?'

William keeps cover.

'Mr Crosby, are you all right? It's the police.'

He hears lowered voices, then the shuffle of footsteps in the hall. A uniformed officer appears in the doorway of his study.

'Mr Crosby?'

William holds onto his bowl. He doesn't know what to say. He isn't sure what is expected of him. Is he in danger? Is this a raid? The young officer already has the buttery face of middle age, a softening chin. He takes a couple of hesitant steps towards William, as if he is approaching a nervous dog. He seems to fill the room. It's another reminder of William's reduced life these days – a bedroom, a kitchen stacked with crockery he's been meaning to wash, a study hemmed in with the clutter of a single man. William notices the policeman's scuffed shoes.

'What do you want?' He is conscious of the soup stains caught in the handkerchief that serves as his napkin.

'Mr Crosby, are you all right, sir?'

William is startled by the humdrum nature of the enquiry. 'You broke into my house to make sure I was all right?'

'You weren't answering your door.'

'I didn't *want* to answer the door.'

'We thought you might be ill, sir. We tried to check whether you were okay through the windows, but we couldn't see you. The blinds in here are drawn.'

'We – who's we?'

'Your son thought you might have collapsed or something. That's why he rang us.'

'My son?'

'He said he called round. He said you haven't been answering your door.'

'It's a crime now if you don't feel like answering the door?'

'I think your son was worried.'

'He couldn't have rung me? He couldn't have *written*?'

'He says he's worried by a letter you wrote him, that you might be unwell.'

'He didn't like it, you mean.'

'He says you don't answer your phone.'

'Sometimes I don't.'

'Is that what's been happening, sir? Your son came round and you've not been letting him in?'

'Is that why you broke my door down? Because I wouldn't answer the door to my son?'

'Did you have an argument with your son, Mr Crosby? Is that why you wouldn't answer the door? He does seem genuinely worried about you.'

'I'm touched, but you can tell my idiot son that I'm fine, thank you.'

'That's not really the point, sir. You really should have let him in. It would have saved a lot of trouble.'

'You want to know what his point was the last time he came? *What's the good of having money sitting in the bank doing nothing?* His point was, *What's the point, when it's coming to him in the end, if some of it could be working for him and Penny now to secure their future.* Well, tell him to write next time he wants to put another business proposition to me, and I'll write back and tell him where he can put his plans for him and Penny. Tell him there is no money.'

'Well, there is some money, Mr Crosby, isn't there?'

'What do you mean?'

'Well, there's an envelope on your doorstep with money in it. Did you know that, sir?'

'There's an envelope?'

'With a bundle of notes sticking out of it. Looks like several hundred pounds. Is it your money, sir?'

'What I do with my money is no concern of anyone's – least of all my son's with his knack for losing the damned stuff.'

'I just need to make sure that you're all right, sir. That no one's taking advantage of you. Did you leave the money there for someone to collect, or was it left for you?'

There is a noise from the kitchen. A door is pushed shut.

'Who's that? There are more of you in here?'

'That'll be your son, sir.'

'Kevin? He's here?'

'He arranged to meet us here. Like I said, you could have been lying ill in here, or worse. We needed to gain access.'

There is a movement in the hall. William's son appears in the doorway. He is holding a carrier bag.

'Christ's sake, Dad, why not just answer your door?'

'Because I didn't want to answer the door.'

'Anything could have happened to you.'

'I could have been eating my soup in peace. I could have been minding my own business.'

'Look, Dad, you're not well. You're not looking after yourself. The house is a pigsty. The kitchen… Jesus, Dad, what would Mum think if she could see you like this?'

'What would she think? If she could see me? Like what? On my own? With my books? Content in my own company? I think Anna would be happy for me to be left in peace.'

'Dad.'

William pulls away the stained handkerchief from his collar and rises slowly to his feet. He rests his standing weight on his cane.

'I think you should leave, now,' he says.

'Oh, for crying out loud.' Kevin turns towards the policeman, appealing over William's head for sanity to prevail. He lobs the carrier bag into the study. It lands solidly on the carpet between the two men.

'He had a dead cat in his fridge,' Kevin says.

'A dead cat?'

'And Mum's name wasn't Anna. It was Margaret.'

16

Tell the truth
Be careful how you tell it
Be careful who you tell it to

WHENEVER I SIT IN THE STUDY, I can generally hear Mum shifting between the kitchen and the sitting room, between the day's pot of soup on the stove and the canvas of winter trees she is working on, or the book she is reading, or the piece of music she is listening to. Sometimes, a piece of cornice, or a crack in the plaster on the wall, will catch her eye and her gaze will settle on it for an hour. In the afternoons, she sometimes sleeps for a while on the sofa. She only uses the study when she needs the computer, and already she has fallen into the habit of asking my permission. Without saying anything, we seem to have reached an agreement that the study is my space. Mine and William's.

The study is my favourite place in the house. When we lived on the avenue, my favourite place was the utility room in the basement, which was warm and muggy when the washer or the dryer were on. I liked to sit and read down there inside the big laundry cupboard, which was full of clean towels and felt like a hammock to climb into with a small pile of books. Here in the farmhouse there is no utility room, and not many places that are terribly warm except right in front of the wood-burning stove. So I wear an extra sweater and spend most of my time in the study.

William's books surround me in the room. My own are now in here, too, squeezed wherever I have been able to fit them alongside William's on the shelves that line the walls. I've had to slot some of them horizontally in twos and threes over the top of his books. I like how his books and mine are now mingled together. I think he would like it like that – maybe not the William who nailed up a sheep's heart to a door, but the one who is standing on the beach in his grey shorts when he was the same age as me. Perhaps when I am old, a young boy will arrange his schoolboy stories alongside the lines of books that I have read and loved and kept throughout my life: everything that Isaac Babel wrote, and everything else that William read, and *Moby Dick*, which my dad bought me once when he was trying to be my friend and which I tried to read and is meant to be a great book, but which I don't really understand. By then, when I am old, I will have had time to read everything, and I will have learned all the things I need to know.

I've never allowed any of my books to be thrown away. I won't let books ever become rubbish. And, apart from Lucas, I've never really known anyone I would choose to give them away to. As a result, all the books I've owned from when I started to read at the age of three – the picture books, the nursery stories with only half a dozen pages, each as solid as wood – are all still in my collection. Whenever I took out a library book and loved it, I would put it on my list of books to buy. 'But you've already read it!' my dad would say, mystified.

The clues that I have so far to William's life have either been ones that I stumbled across by accident (the letters he was drafting, the nailing up of the sheep's heart), or they were sitting there waiting for me, not needing any skill on my part (the shoes, the photograph of William as a boy). But I've now decided that it makes sense to carry out a more detailed search of the house, one room at a time, starting at ground level and working up. I begin in the outhouse, then move indoors to work in turn through each of the ground-floor rooms. I have to carry out my examination of the sitting room in stages to make sure Mum doesn't realize what I am doing. I don't want her worrying about me. I don't want her thinking I'm getting obsessive about William, like she thinks I sometimes do about other things. I manage to get half the living-room search done while she is finishing off the soup for lunch, and the other half while she is seeing to the van driver who parks up in the yard to deliver the supermarket shopping that she ordered online earlier in the week.

By the time the search is complete, I have half-filled one of the 'Contents for Burning' cardboard boxes I retrieved from the outhouse with things that escaped the attention of William's son in his own trawl of the house. There is an old cigarette lighter, some more photographs, a collection of school reports for William's children, an invitation to a regimental reunion forwarded to him by a man called Joseph Brody who seemed to know William in the war, a seed catalogue with William's notes in the margins, several planting plans for the vegetables in the kitchen garden, a box of Amitriptyline (which Google says are sleeping tablets), an assortment of keys in a metal tea caddy, his expired passport and driving licence from a shelf in his wardrobe.

In the bedroom that was William's, that is now mine, I pin his passport and driving licence to the pale wall on which I have already attached the letter to his daughter and the photograph of William on the beach as a boy. I sit down at the dressing table. One by one, I fish out the keys from the tea caddy and try them in the keyhole in the drawer beneath the mirror. None of them fits. I scoop the keys back into the caddy and take them and my other finds downstairs to the study.

I sit at the desk, looking at the new photographs. Two of them are of the house. The black and white photographs make the farmhouse look neglected. This must be how William found it when he first came here and decided to buy the house. The other photographs are family snaps – children playing, feeding a goat, on holiday on a beach somewhere. William, the family man, with his two children either side of him, looks slightly away from the camera like he did at the age of eleven. Could he remember then, halfway through his life, posing beside his son and daughter, what it was like to be eleven and standing alone on a beach?

I reach across to the back of the desk for the typewriter that still mis-positions its 'c's the way it did each time for William. It's heavier than a laptop, but simple enough to lift. Gently, I turn it over. I don't know why. Taped to the inside is a narrow brass key. I peel the tape off and hold the key up to the light. Upstairs in the bedroom, it slips without fuss into the keyhole of the dressing-table drawer. I slide the drawer open. Inside is a large, fat envelope. It is addressed to William. There is a line of foreign stamps beneath the postmark. I open the envelope and lift out the contents. I put them on my knee. I'm holding a wad of letters held together with a bulldog clip. I remember the letter I found in the desk: *We are instructed by the Singer family to return all the enclosed communications as the hotel is closing down, and we regret that no further assistance can be offered.* I can feel my score going up a little to 5.2.

The first letter, dated 8th February 1947, is on paper that is dry and yellowing. Some of the letters consist of just a few sentences, others run to several sides. Each of the letters, at the end, is signed 'William'. Each time a 'c' is typed on any of the pages, it tilts backwards and sits below the line of the other letters. The last letter was sent three years ago.

Here are pieces of his life that were not gathered up in the cardboard boxes, not harvested for burning. Not yet anyway.

I Google 'Lienz'. The computer says the address – the one on the letter sent by the man called Emile on behalf of the Singer family – is in Austria. On the screen I bring up a map showing that the town of Lienz is near the Italian border. Perhaps that means William wasn't a spy after the war, because Austria was in the West, not part of the communist bloc that Mum said we spied on after World War Two.

I text Lucas.

Today, we saw a woman carrying a small Pekingese in her arm across the lobby of the hotel and one of the bellboys shouted, 'Duchess, we have a letter for you!' Also, did you know a dumb waiter is just a small lift in a hotel for carrying food up from the kitchen?

I go to bed early. I start to read the first of the letters I found when I unlocked the drawer. 'My dearest girl,' it says. 'I have seen heaven. It is a real place.'

17

WILLIAM CAN HEAR THEM afterwards, out in the yard – the two policemen, one of whom had waited outside, and William's son. The three of them share professional confidences, swapping tales of ageing and troublesome parents.

The two policemen have wedged the frame back in place, so that at least the front door is secure for now, but the lock and a piece of the casing need replacing. William sits on the floor in the hallway with his back against the door where he slumped after marching the two men to the door and slamming it behind them. Outside, his son is speaking. His son the accountant, the man with the financial foresight to ensure that the money he had worked so diligently to keep clear of his ex-wife had all but disappeared in the black hole of some offshore investment scheme that went wrong.

He thinks of Kevin as having only two dimensions – everything easily containable on a balance sheet. To the policemen who have broken down his father's door, though, Kevin is the metropolitan man of the world, a man in a good suit and a checked overcoat, who has interrupted the general running order of his professional life with as much good grace as he can muster to attend to the business of his failing father.

'What did he do?' one of them says. 'Before all this?'

There is a crackle of static from the police walkie-talkies.

All what? William wonders from behind the door. A dead cat and a soup stain?

'He was a teacher,' he hears Kevin say. 'Grammar school. Head of the history department.'

'Is this where you grew up?'

'It's the back of beyond, isn't it? Snow every winter for weeks, no mains gas, no central heating. Mum hated it, but he wouldn't ever hear of moving.'

'Do you think he's changed? His personality? People do as they get older.'

'Do you mean was he always so welcoming?'

There is a snort of laughter.

'I always tell people if they ask about him,' Kevin says, 'that there are probably only three things you need to know to get to the heart of my father. If you know them, you're home and dry. One is that every night of his life, years after the instincts of his army basic training must have melted away, even after he retired from teaching, whether or not he had someone to see or was even leaving the house, he had to polish his shoes ready for the morning. Christ, for all I know he still does. Then there's the challenge of not being good enough for him. My mum said that after I was born, he was obsessed with having a daughter. There's ten years between me and my sister. Before Becky came along, I think he'd given up on having a girl. By then, even I had recognized that I was just a consolation. I think my mother was, too. Afterwards, neither of us could ever be good enough. Becky was the one, and look how that ended.'

'Why do you say that?'

'About Becky? She and my father haven't spoken properly since she was about nineteen. A bit of freedom at university and she was away. There was a huge row one Christmastime when she came back and they haven't had anything much to do with each other since. I suppose the last time they saw each other was at my mother's funeral ten years ago.'

'So what was the third thing?'

'The third thing? Oh, yeah, the third thing. I tell people

that my father believed there are more ways to mess up your life than you can shake a stick at, but that people get only one shot at real happiness. That was one of his mantras. He had plenty of them. After we stopped listening to him, he resorted to hurling his pieces of wisdom at my mother. You made one mistake in my father's eyes and that was it – he was done with you for ever.'

With his back pressed against the splintered frame of the front door, William sits motionless. His visitors have long since gone back down the hill. He is sapped by the matter-of-factness of his son's betrayal of him to strangers. Is he so easily dismissed? Is that the sum of his parts? As he sits in the hallway, his face is fixed. His eyes are unfocused. He is recalling, as if it were six months ago, the noise of the wind slapping the side of the farmhouse on his first night here after they moved in. A thousand feet up in the hills, the ancient stone had stood firm. With Margaret gone to bed, he had remained at the big table in the kitchen until the small hours. He felt at peace. He recalled how it had felt lying in the cot at the hospital in Milan in which he slept on and off for three days, refusing food, wondering when Brody would turn up, watching the flaking plaster beneath the picture rail, listening to the constant rain dripping outside the hospital window from a damaged spout. The storm in the Pennine hills that first night had gradually slackened and blown itself away. Only slowly, as the recollection fades, do William's features lose their rigidity. His face collapses gently into grief, his hands clutching fast the carrier bag with the dead cat inside.

18

Play marbles
Joseph Brody?
Whether you could jump from one part of the universe to another through a wormhole

Dear Mr Crosby,

I got your email address from the estate agent you are using to sell your father's house. My name is de Bruin, and we are renting Bank Hey Farm from you. We have found some letters in your father's desk that he had typed out. The estate agent said he thought your father had had a stroke, so I don't think he got a chance to post them. One of the letters is for your sister, Rebecca. Do you have an email address so we can contact her about it? Also, I don't know if your father died or if he is still alive. If he is alive, I have some questions for him about the farm which is quite an interesting place, if you don't think he would mind.

Yours sincerely,
M de Bruin

Here's the thing. When Wile E. Coyote is chasing Road Runner in the old cartoons and he goes off the edge of the cliff, he keeps on running in mid-air until he looks down and realizes there's nothing beneath him.

I used to think that's what would happen. I believed that, as long as you didn't look down, you would be able to carry on running like Wile E. Coyote did. I remember wondering whether, if you had enough momentum, you could hold your arms out and just float quite nicely for a short stretch, like the driver of a car taking his foot off the accelerator, before starting to run again. But then, I thought, how hard would it be not to look down? You would want so much to glance down, just for a split second, to see yourself running like that through the air with nothing solid beneath you, but the moment you did that, as Max happily pointed out, you would fall like a stone, and he did an impersonation of a stone falling that made me and Lucas laugh.

'It's just a cartoon,' Max said. 'They can make anything happen in a cartoon.'

I felt cheated.

But he falls in the end, I wrote.

I get a long text from Lucas. *Mouse*, it says, *can't you give me the address of the hotel you're staying in? I'd really like to write a proper letter. I miss not coming to your house. I miss Max and I'm really sorry that he died, and I'd like to be able to write stuff down sometimes and send it to you down in London. Is that okay? It would be a really good thing if I could. Lucas.*

I make a chocolate roulade. Mum eats a piece after her tea. She says it's the best roulade she's ever eaten.

How many times have you had it before? I ask.

She smiles. I make a note that this evening she is 3.9, which is pretty good for her.

Dear Lucas,

The flies infesting our house here in London are proving stubborn to get rid of. They have spread from the attic to the bedrooms, so we have moved to a new hotel just until they have been dealt with. Once again I'm not sure how many days we'll be here, but I'm sure it'll all get sorted soon. Then

I'll be able to give you a more permanent address you can write to. Our new hotel doesn't overlook the River Thames. It's in a quieter street, and this time we don't have doormen. I think it's less expensive for Mum's firm in case we need to stay here for several more days. The walls are thinner in this hotel. Sometimes I can hear the voices of the guests in other rooms as we pass by. The staff are mostly foreign young people. They are very formal and polite, and they speak good English, but their uniforms are not so stylish. Some of them look a little pale and quite a few have frayed collars on their shirts. The food is good, but not so many people eat in the dining room of this new hotel, so Mum and I have the pick of where we want to sit. I believe that's all for now.

Yours truly,
Mouse

Three or four times, Mum took me to watch a case in which she was involved. I liked watching her in the courtroom. I liked the idea of other people seeing her not as my mum but as a person called Caroline de Bruin who was, to them, a barrister who also happened to have two children.

She was careful about the kind of cases she took me to see, especially since her job was to defend people, some of whom were accused of serious things. I suppose she had to consider whether it was appropriate for a girl of nine or ten – someone who *didn't even have a voice* – to be sitting in a courtroom. But she seemed pleased that I wanted to go, and just occasionally, if I wasn't at school and if I'd been asking to go, she would let me sit at the back of the public gallery and would arrange for the usher to keep an eye on me. I think she'd decided that it was more likely than not to be a positive experience. It was a chance to see how a court in session worked. And perhaps it was an opportunity, in Mum's mind at least, for me to begin to consider the law as a career when I was older, and when my voice had returned.

The first time I went, I realized as I watched the case unfold, as witnesses came and went, that I wasn't sure who was telling the truth and who wasn't.

Do you know? I wrote down for Mum that night.

'Not always,' she said. 'My job is to represent my client, but I always hope the case will have the right outcome.'

But what if someone is lying? I wrote.

She thought about it. 'That's what the jury have to decide,' she said. 'Their job is to listen to the evidence, and to make up their minds about who they think is lying and who is telling the truth.'

I asked Mum why they didn't just make everyone have a lie detector test as they were giving their evidence. *That way*, I wrote, *the jury would* ***know*** *who was telling the truth*. Mum laughed and said, 'Ah, little Mouse,' and explained how lie detector tests measure a person's heart rate and perspiration and finger twitching and so on, but they can't actually tell you definitively if someone is *lying*. That's why they aren't admissible as evidence in a court. Who knows – maybe if they hooked my dad up to a lie detector machine to measure his heart rate and his perspiration and so on, and said, 'Did you love Caroline de Bruin as much as she loved you?' he'd say, 'Sure I did,' in his *that's a dumb question* kind of way, and the machine would whirr away and he would whizz through the test.

I've seen lie detector tests being carried out in a couple of the films Lucas and I went to see with his mum. The interrogator always starts with a few simple questions to establish a baseline for truthful answers. *Beep, beep, beep* the machine goes. It beeps and jigs and hums, recording the data before its findings are analysed to indicate if someone is lying or not. There are plenty of questions where the answers are obvious that someone doing a lie detector test could ask me. They could ask me if Mum likes soup: I know she does because she makes it all the time. They could ask me if Mum loves me, and if she loved Max, and if she loved my dad for a long, long time, and it would be easy to answer 'yes' to all these questions, and the machine would *beep beep* away to say I was telling the truth each time. If they tested Lucas, they could ask him if his name was Lucas Greaves, or if he likes lemon poppy seed muffins, and he would say 'yes' and the machine would hum happily. But then I wonder what would happen if they wired Mum up to test her. As they started, they might ask what the date was, or whether it was Tuesday today, and that would be fine. But if they said to her, 'Are you Caroline de Bruin?' I think that question might make her hesitate. I think she'd have to sit there, all connected up to the sensors with the little wires transmitting information about her heart rate and blood pressure and perspiration to the machine, trying to work out, as best she could, how much of Caroline de Bruin she still is. I don't know if she believes there is enough of her left to be certain that this is who she is. And all the time she was sat there, trying to work this out in her head, the machine would be going *beep, beep, beep*. It would feel like the moment when Wile E. Coyote is still hurtling along at top speed but has run out of road, and he's having to decide whether he should look down beneath him or try to keep on running.

19

My dear girl,

Where to start? How to start? Not with the obvious, perhaps. Sometimes it seems best to come at things sideways on. I should start, I think, with Herr Singer's library – and with the clumsiness of my fingers striking at the lighter.

To be surrounded by books in silence seemed like a benediction. It barely mattered that most of the books were in German or French. It mattered even less that the library, in a wing of the Singers' Tyrolean hotel, had lost half of its defining shape – no roof, one wall reduced to rubble. What is more natural than a room holding rows of Goethe and Baudelaire being open to the stars? For three days (and nights) now, the room had become my bolt-hole.

The damage was the result of a jettisoned bomb from an Allied air raid, which had fallen on the stable block. The blast had reduced the side wall and part of the library's ceiling to rubble. On the fringes of the remaining portion of the room, the books were now gently mouldering after the winter rains. To pick one up was to feel the binding and its pages part like cake. Even the shelves of undamaged volumes further back inside the room were still coated in a fine filth of dust and soot.

There had been no attempt to clean up the damage, to salvage the books. The Singers had simply cordoned off the wing and declared it out of bounds, at the time to the handful of guests in that final winter of the war, and now to the forward battalions of 36th Brigade, some of whom had been billeted in the hotel two days ago after our unopposed push into Austria from northern Italy through the Plöckenpass.

I was trying to coax a flame from the lighter. I was telling myself that the flint had worn smooth, or had been dislodged, but the challenge, in truth, was more about encouraging my fingers to do as they were bid. Every now and then I gave them a break and allowed my eyes to slide along the rows of books.

The lighter had belonged to a German. It was Brody who had retrieved it from the man's body. When, the following winter, I returned from my two weeks in the hospital outside Milan complaining that I had lost my own lighter, he seemed happy enough to offer it to me.

Brody and I had been together more or less since Sicily. It was the only thing we had in common. Everything else argued against our friendship. For one thing, he was braver than me in his *Boy's Own* adventure way. And he had replaced Carlisle, who I had liked very much. His parents, Brody said, had been missionaries in China, and when he was younger he had considered joining the Presbyterian ministry. He didn't drink, and had a touching belief in a God who seemed on close personal terms with both his parents. I, on the other hand, had no such convictions. There was, as well, I suppose, an unspoken distance we had learned to keep from each other. An instinct had developed not to form too close a bond with colleagues around you who might, in a heartbeat, in a turn of the head, step onto a mine or walk into a sniper's line of fire.

I think Brody enjoyed the war more than I did. A Scottish public school education accounted, it seems, for his enthusiasm for the Argentinian liver we were routinely fed in the mess tent, which arrived frozen in vast, veiny blocks, which were sliced and then boiled for much of the day in an effort to make the food palatable. The same education had also equipped him for the privations of war. Those damp dormitories, dawn cross country runs and the relentlessly enforced optimism of boarding school life had turned him into a natural soldier who was good at games and who slept soundly every night. In civilian life, I suspect we would have been happy to cross the road to avoid each other. But war had forced us into an alliance that had bred a tolerance of the other's foibles.

Brody and I had been allocated an attic room together in the staff quarters of the hotel on the edge of Lienz, which was run by the Singers and their two remaining staff. The room was big enough for the two of us to move around in peaceably as long as we remembered, like dancers, to move in hold. Brody, being six foot three and a noisy sleeper, added to the challenge. It was in escaping from his snoring on the first night that I stumbled upon what was left of the library as I wandered the corridors, picking out the way with my flashlight.

That evening, Brody had come back to the room to shave. He was anxious for me to walk down with him into the town. As I remember it, this might even have been the day the fighting stopped, what we would later think of as VE Day. There was, by all account, some reason to celebrate something or other. Brody had been told the Cossacks were playing balalaikas and there was dancing in the square. He was adamant that we really should go.

I seem to think I had been lying on the bed struggling to read.

'You go,' I told him. 'I haven't done my laundry in weeks.'

He gave me one of his schoolboy looks before trying one further throw of the dice. 'Your woman may be there.'

'My woman?'

'Ach, you know. The interpreter. I saw you looking at her when we met them at HQ. You should get in there tonight before some horny bloody Glaswegian makes a move.'

'I thank you for your wise counsel.'

He shrugged, determined that even Captain Crosby's

English recidivism would not deflect him from the promise of an evening's entertainment. He offered me the unexpired portion of his daily ration. I declined and laid back on the bed.

When I woke, he had gone. I had been left for company with the tin of bully beef and Brody's week-old *Daily Mirror*. The room still smelled of petrol from his earlier attempts to get his uniform decently clean using the dregs of a five-gallon fuel can. I thought about how much a cigarette would help. Rather than demonstrate more bravery than was strictly necessary on what may well have been the first day of peace, I chose to try my luck at striking a spark in the library and to sit for a while amongst Herr Singer's volumes and the evening sky.

It was a couple of hours later, I suppose, when with the light fading I walked down into the town. The road into Lienz ran against a steep backdrop of forest. I could hear the rush of the River Drau running fast near by. Beyond the town, it was possible to see the fires of the Cossack encampment trailing away into the distance.

In the town square, just as Brody had promised, some of the Cossacks, officers mainly, had come in to play music and to drink. There were balalaikas and accordions playing. One of the Argyles had brought into the square a set of bagpipes. Waiters from the hotel in the square were serving beer and schnapps to groups of people sat at the outside tables. Taking in the scene, it seemed possible to believe that the world had, finally, come to its senses.

I found Anna on the far side of the square, sitting at a table with three older men and one young, silent companion. The young man had an impressive scar down one cheek running past his big Russian lips. He wore a nondescript military tunic and was paying close attention to the others but contributing nothing. All three older men had heavy, yellow beards and wore riding boots. One of them I recognized from earlier in the day as Vasilenko, the colonel, who, according to Anna, had fought alongside her father for the White Army against the Bolsheviks in the civil war that followed the revolution. The other two wore wolf-skin caps. As if not entirely confident of the new peace, the three of them wore rows of cartridge cases across each side of their chests. Locked in conversation around the table, observed intently by the young scar-faced man, these three were all gestures and sighs. It seemed possible to me, in my distracted state, that here were men who may have come direct from facing down the Emperor Napoleon at Borodino.

What struck me about Anna, sat slightly apart from this group at the table, was her poise. I stood and watched her happily for a while until she caught sight of me. She stood up and beckoned me over to sit with them. There was another rapid conversation between the four of them that I could not understand. Vasilenko rose.

'Crosby, sit, sit! Here!'

He poured vodka from a bottle on the table into a spare tumbler and gestured at a chair. As he continued speaking with the others, Anna smiled.

'The colonel is telling the others that you are an important man.'

'Why would he think that? I'm a captain, for God's sake.'

'He is explaining that Colonel Malcolm has appointed you as the liaison officer for the Cossack settlement in the valley. He has said you will be our voice in helping us to deal honourably with the British.'

Vasilenko finished speaking to his comrades. He gestured to the vacant chair I had still not taken. 'So now, you will sit with us and drink, Crosby, yes? And then I think Anna will drive you out to see the camp.'

'This late?' I queried.

'Late? This is surely the beginning of the night? A great night. We have things to celebrate – all of us.'

Brody and I had met Anna and Colonel Vasilenko for the first time that afternoon in Colonel Malcolm's newly established HQ in Lienz, along with General Domanov who was commanding the Cossacks. And so I sat with them at their table on the edge of the square and drank, and they told me their story, and I avoided telling them mine – that, after my return from the hospital in Milan, I suspected there was little else the brigade could think to give me to do other than to nursemaid an eccentric refugee camp in the hills now that my company had been reconfigured and the war was over.

It was approaching midnight when we set out from the square in a large Fiat touring saloon, the kind that sported running boards and a high roof, which Vasilenko himself had impounded for the journey over the Plöckenpass. The car had been parked in a side street close to the square. When we reached it, I was surprised to see a child, maybe eight or nine years old, covered by a greatcoat and asleep on the back seat.

'That is Leo,' Anna said. 'Don't worry. He sleeps like a winter bear. Nothing will wake him until the morning.'

'Is he yours?'

'No, no. He lost his parents. He travels with us now. He seems to have adopted me. I look after him, and he makes sure there is enough food on our table and runs errands for the colonel.'

Anna drove, the boy slept soundly in the back, and I sat in the passenger seat looking out of the window.

'Where did you learn your English?' I asked.

'After the Bolsheviks triumphed,' she said, 'my family lived in exile, in Berlin and then in Yugoslavia. We spoke English there. By the time war broke out, I had started working in Yugoslavia for Standard Oil.'

She was compact, dark-haired, bare-armed. She seemed competent and serene. Although younger than me, she appeared wiser in a way I couldn't quite pin down. Beyond the car, campfires, tents, wagons and horses filled the outline of meadow after meadow. Anna told me that the Cossacks had waged war relentlessly on the Bolsheviks in the struggle for control after 1917. They formed an important part of the White Armies, she said, whose cause in the ensuing civil war Winston Churchill, as Britain's secretary for war, had energetically supported. They had treated the German army in 1940 as liberators of their lands from Soviet communism, but Germany's retreat after Stalingrad meant the Cossacks were compelled to fall back with them to avoid annihilation at the hands of Stalin's vengeful thugs. Forty thousand of them – families, children, carts heavy with their possessions, horses, an entire race of people – retreated west for months through the Russian steppes and the lands of eastern Europe. They were deposited by the Germans in northern Italy before moving once more in the final days of the war from their camp at Tolmezzo over the mountains into Austria to escape the hostile attentions of Italian partisans and the advancing Allies.

'The generals have great faith in the British,' Anna said. 'They had to decide whether to talk to the British or the Americans about our predicament. They discussed this with Colonel Vasilenko, and they chose the British.'

We had won that particular raffle, it seemed, because of the high regard in which the Cossacks held Churchill, and because Vasilenko and Anna's father had fought with Field Marshal Alexander himself against the Bolsheviks. The Cossacks, Anna emphasized, had no quarrel with the Allies. Their struggle had been against the Bolsheviks, who had waged a war against the Cossack lands. Many of them, it seemed from Anna, anticipated that, in its defence of nationhood, the West would turn on Stalin now that the Germans were defeated, and the Cossacks were keen to fight alongside the Allies in this next stage of the war.

We drove on through the valley and still there were more of them. At one point we passed a field full of camels that the Cossacks had brought with them. Anna saw my face and smiled. It was true, it seemed, that an entire race had descended on the Drau valley in a scene of biblical proportion.

She talked about her people. 'We want asylum in the free world,' she said. 'We want to live as a people. To settle in the West, in a civilized world, and the British will help us to do this'

I thought of the Italian grandmothers I had seen in the lanes around Mignano chiselling gold teeth from dead German soldiers; piano wire strung across the roads behind the Gustav Line casually decapitating motorcyclists. I thought of Carlisle in search of eggs pulling back the door of a booby-trapped hen house. I thought: your people have walked a thousand miles to be part of this? But each time I glanced across at her as she drove I could see that it was true, that this people amongst whom I was being driven believed it was possible for them, now the war was over, to start again in a new land, to escape their past and live their lives in a free world; and Anna Kirov seemed the embodiment of that hope.

You must understand, my dear girl, that she and I had one crucial thing in common. Against all logic, we had done what Carlisle had not; what two hundred thousand men fighting for possession of a sixth-century monastery at Cassino had not. We had both survived unscathed. The worst was over. We believed this. I believed this. She drove on, past further miles of her compatriots in tents in fields waiting patiently for their new life in the West to begin. I thought of the flight of the Israelites from Egypt. Until that night I had come to believe that I believed in nothing. Now I realized that I believed in her.

20

WITH BOTH HANDS WILLIAM lifts one final stone, positions it in place, then reaches for his stick. And then there is a jump in time. Some frames have been cut from the spool that is projecting his life. That's how it feels. One minute he is leaning towards his stick, the next he is lying on the ground a little distance away. The two moments are disconnected. The smell of recently dug earth fills his head. His face is pressed to the soil. His legs are twisted together, as though in those few frames they have developed a life of their own. But in that time they have ceased to be his legs. He cannot move.

'Fuck,' he means to say, but something different leaks from his bent mouth. He can lift his left hand, but no other part of his body will respond to his commands. How is this possible? He has an urge to plead that this is a mistake, that it shouldn't have happened. He was only lifting a few stones. He has moved hundreds of stones over dozens of years. The raised bed running down the side of the walled garden had finally buckled after a winter of ice picking at the mortar in the joints. He simply wanted to rearrange a few stones. He could have waited for Anthony. He had walked down the field to open the gate. That was the signal for Anthony. If the gate was open, Anthony could make his way up the field to spend the day helping William in the walled garden; if the gate was closed, William wanted no company and Anthony should go back home. That was the deal William had struck with Anthony's mother, Mary, after the incident with the dead cat. He could have waited for Anthony, who would have been happy to carry stones around all day for William, but it was only a few stones. It was a minor repair.

As Mary Challener, William had known her as a bright girl, but she had worn her cleverness lightly. It seemed to surprise her. He remembered her as a Betjeman kind of girl – big-boned and pretty in a fresh-faced, unsophisticated English way. A netball player and, surprisingly for the local comprehensive school, a potential candidate for Oxbridge.

For perhaps a term, forty years ago, William had tutored her two evenings a week at the farm. He'd been approached by Mary's mother, who knew that William taught at the grammar school in Bury, knew also that his school had a track record of getting pupils into Oxford and Cambridge. She asked if William would tutor Mary in the lead-up to her entrance exam. She offered a rate that was enough for him to say yes. Teachers in those far-off days were well respected, but not well paid. So he agreed.

In the years after that, he caught sight of Mary occasionally. He knew about the pregnancy that had derailed her ambitions, about the mongol son she had produced, the marriage to the local boy who was the father, the separation that came months after a second child. But the town was just big enough and William private enough, hidden sufficiently away on his land up on the hill, to keep them apart. People's paths connect, run parallel for a while and then drift apart. He had grown used to this in the army. He was accustomed to it happening at the school with its yearly turnover of pupils and staff who jostled daily for his attention, filled his thinking time, then vanished without trace. And so it had surprised him when it turned out that the terraced front door to which he had nailed the sheep's pluck belonged to Mary Challener, now Beale, and that Anthony was her adult, firstborn son.

At their first tutorial, William had recognized that Mary was a capable rather than an outstanding scholar – he was teaching brighter students than her at the grammar school – but he marked her down as someone who would move on, make something of herself. When they met each Tuesday and Thursday for those weeks in his study, he watched amused as she wrestled with the questions that he posed her. Years later, watching his own daughter, Rebecca, wrestle with the knowledge she was eager to master and which came more easily to her, William was sometimes reminded of Mary Challener and her earnest summer seeking wisdom under his tutelage.

As a child, William's daughter had lived in her own world. It was a strong interior life that sustained Rebecca even as a toddler, a place into which, in her early years, William had routinely been granted entry. She could make up games, entertain herself with acts of imagination, in a way that had always been beyond poor, literal-minded Kevin. For want of a better phrase, Rebecca had a spark. William rejoiced in it, encouraged it, and her loyalty to him seemed absolute. In the flagged kitchen, the room nestled in the warmth seeping from the vast and ancient range, she would sit on his lap and whisper: 'Tell me a secret, Daddy.' They played make-believe, inventing worlds that just the two of them understood. They worked on the vegetable plot in the walled garden that he had created twenty years before. He read to her, she read for him. Her thirst for knowledge was endless. She wrote him stories. They performed outdoor plays with only the caged rabbits and the glassy-eyed goat as their audience. How could he have produced someone so remarkable, so precious? How had he earned such blessings? How could he prevent harm from befalling her? How could a creature so slight, so seemingly fragile, be expected to survive the world that lay in wait for her?

Just once, up at the farm, a journalist had turned up wanting to talk to him about Rebecca. It was a year or so after William's wife had died. Rebecca's decisive act of rebellion against him at nineteen was still, years later, an open and weeping sore. He had sent the man packing. Standing in the yard, the journalist had told William he was doing a profile because the play Becky was acting in down in London was doing well. He named the paper, a broadsheet. The piece was for their weekend magazine supplement. William had threatened to set the dog on him. When the piece appeared it made a brief reference to him as a recluse. It described Becky as 'estranged' from her father.

William had known about the play. He had followed the stages of her career, the theatre, the television, her marriage breakdown, her seemingly contented relationship since then with a theatre director. But not her addresses, her phone numbers, her favourite places, her real life. All of this was unknown. All this a blank. So many blanks. Such absences. And, for the first time, he catches a glimpse of the true shape of his life in which it is the absences that have given it form, exerting a moon-like gravity on him as they orbit what is left of his life, silently, relentlessly, invisible to the naked eye.

His face is pressed to the earth. His body remains inert. There is a loop of memory running over and over in his head. It is the episode of the sheep's pluck. As it runs, he cannot empty himself of the sound of his son's voice. He hears Kevin's disdain being uttered over his unresponding limbs like a cinematic voiceover.

'... Sheep's entrails, nailed to the door, of a handicapped man ... yes, a man who had brought the cat back for him!'

What had struck William most about the pluck as he inspected the organs he had bought for the express purpose of pinning to the boy's front door – the heart, lungs, liver – was their crudeness. It was the lack of their apparent potential for anything other than the pot. He was amazed that these paltry things had enough in them to power a living beast. He found himself considering his own functioning organs. Did the consultant who had delivered his prognosis view William's own diseased body with the same dispassionate contempt? No need for the man to look his eleven o'clock patient in the eye, William supposed, if he was nothing more to him than perishable meat.

It was the two pieces of the cat that had so upset him. It was the way a sentient creature had been, not so neatly, halved. He had no problem with eating meat. He had never been vaguely moved by the arguments of the vegetarian movement. But, in the case of the cat, it was the futility of the act that had forced him to respond. Its destruction had served no purpose other than to shock him; to goad; to taunt. We have done this thing, the act said, because we can. This is the mark we choose to make upon the world. We have acted, and you will not respond, and because of it we now have dominion over you. Everything – your field, your outhouse, your cat, your grief – exists for no other purpose than for our sullen, dull-eyed, sniggering entertainment each time we choose to trespass across your land. And so, because he had entered this final phase, an age of reckoning, where it was necessary for everything to be rounded off, where wrongs needed to be righted, and where all truths should be revealed in order that he could be sure of reaching the end emptied and resolved, he had gone to the butcher's in the town and bought the sheep's pluck and hung it on the door of the house of the presumed perpetrator.

However hard William tries, the spool will not rewind. He cannot shift Kevin's mockery from inside his head. He cannot wind back the film of the last twenty minutes of his life to reach a point just before he started lifting the final stone when he could stand upright and face the word. He cannot undo what is done. Instead, he lies ridiculously in the dirt of his Camelot, his fortress intended to keep him safe for ever from the abominations of the world, waiting for Anthony and his uncurious face to appear. There is soil in his nostrils from the rise in the ground where he has fallen that he alone knows conceals the two halves of the dead cat.

21

IN THE LETTER MARY sent William telling him that it was the Kelly boys who had killed his cat, she explained who she was – that as a girl, a woman almost, she had been tutored by him one summer. Did he perhaps remember? She said that Anthony was her son.

'I acted in haste,' his reply said, tucked into an envelope with the money he offered. 'Please consider accepting, so we can regard the matter as closed.'

She walked up from the town to return the package with his money in, leaving it on his doorstep. It was too fat to push through the letterbox. It was the first time she had been up to the farm since she was eighteen.

When she returned the money a second time, the note he sent her said, 'Surely there must be some way to make amends?' That was when she had proposed that he might consider letting Anthony help out occasionally on his land. She would not take his money but she would accept such an arrangement as recompense. She said Anthony liked being busy, enjoyed being outdoors. She told him that social services had closed the day centre and there was nothing much for him to do except spend his days avoiding the Kelly brothers.

They agreed the deal standing stiffly across his doorstep – the middle-aged woman still responsible for her two grown sons and the old man alone in his farmhouse above the town. She walked away, the business concluded.

◆ ◆ ◆

It occurred to Mary that she had spent her life mastering the art of stillness.

It had become a kind of purpose, the way some people worked to perfect the use of watercolours, or the playing of the piano. It kept her out of reach. When the pains came as she had given birth to each of her sons, to Anthony and then to Luke, she had fought not for the release of screams, or the hurling of obscenities across the delivery room, but for the purity of containment. To give nothing away became the key. It was the last line of her defence.

A couple of times her control gave way to uncontained fury. Once at the boy who had fathered her two sons and then walked away (at twenty, he seemed a boy, too); once at a solicitor in whose office she worked and whose sexual advances she had rejected at the firm's Christmas party who was (very sadly, he explained) having to make her redundant as part of the new year belt-tightening process.

These explosions, when they came, had astonished her even as they were unfolding. It was as though someone else was responsible, as if an actor had taken her place and Mary herself was a bystander. She remembered each tiny detail of these incidents, even now, years later.

And so, as each slam of the hammer sounded on her front door and rattled the frame of the house, and the nail was driven further in by her (at that stage) unknown assailant, she sat quite still, gripping the arm of the chair, until there was silence again. Until the storm had passed. Only later did she learn from a neighbour across the road, who had been watching from her bedroom window, that it was William Crosby of all people who had punched the nail into her door, and Mary wondered how she would begin to write about this.

22

I LOOK UP AND SEE A HOLE in the cloud, a small piece of blue in a grey Pennine day. I push my glasses up my nose, lower my head again and resume my work, kneeling, facing the long line of the vegetable plot. I pick out another weed with a hand that's already numb with cold. The earth around its root crumbles in my fingers. The soil in the garden is black, gentle stuff. I wonder how many years it took to make it like this. I wonder what William felt when he was finally forced to leave his garden. The lines of last summer's exhausted runner beans up ahead of me hang like dried straw from the patchwork of canes. Pale grey cabbages have holes like cheeses running through them now that the slugs have taken their fill. The stalks of late potatoes lie soft and matted on the ground. I don't suppose he meant for that to happen. I don't think he intended for there to be an end to all this.

On my knees I shuffle down the plot inch by inch, pulling out last year's unharvested crop, scraping back the winter moss in handfuls from the surface of the ground, like peeling the skin off custard. Gradually my neck starts to stiffen and plead for release. I begin to wonder, once I've finished weeding, how long it will take to dig the patch, how many hours before the soil is ready for planting? I imagine pressing the spade to the ground, putting my foot on the shoulder of the blade, pushing, feeling it slide into the earth, then turning it. There – the first one done.

The rain has drifted in off the moor. It makes no sound as

it falls, misting my glasses. When I raise my head to look above the walls enclosing me I can see the tops of the three trees that stand guard over the paddock. From the tallest one I watch a solitary crow taking to the air. It glides towards the copse at the bottom of the field, disappears from view, then rises bravely a few moments later with a thread of twig in its beak.

Dear Mr Brody,

I hope you don't mind me contacting you. I have your name and address because I am related to William Crosby, who I believe you know. He was in the middle of writing a long letter to you when he had a stroke that you might already know about. If it is all right, I want to ask you three things.

1. Do you want me to send you the letter William wrote to you but didn't get the chance to post?
2. Would you be willing to answer some questions about William? Email would be good if you have a computer.
3. William wrote a lot of letters to someone that he sent to a hotel in an Austrian town. He seemed to write quite a few letters a year for most of his life. Do you know who he was writing them to? Do you know why he was writing them?

Yours sincerely,
Ms M de Bruin

How Schrodinger's cat might be alive and not alive at the same time
Stopping slugs eating lettuce
Where texted words are exactly when they're between the phone sending them and the one receiving them

I feel better after my bath. It's dark now outside and the house lights are on. Mum's in the kitchen – I can hear her. I sit in the study cutting a small circular shape from the centre of a photograph. It's of me and Max standing on either side of my dad. It was taken by Mum in the garden of our house on the avenue. My hand gripping the scissors feels sore from the weeding I did all day. My wrist aches in the place where it was broken last year in the crash, the way it still does whenever I lift heavy things. My knees are stiff. My shoulders hurt. Part of the nail from my right index finger came off, and my thumbnail cracked down the middle when it caught a stone as I scooped up a handful of moss. Both times it happened I yelled out, which was stupid of me. When it started to rain I put up my anorak hood and carried on. I saw a crow building its nest in the rain one twig at a time. I walked through into the paddock to watch the bird. I looked down the field and saw the man-boy at the gate, waiting, arms threaded through the bars.

Last night in bed I kept turning, not sleeping. I got up and tried using the telescope but the sky was too cloudy. I could have switched the light on and read, or gone downstairs to see if Mum was awake and making soup, but instead I lay there in the shadows thinking of the ruined garden. This morning I announced to Mum that I was going to clear the ground in the walled garden.

'How about working on a small part of the plot?' she said. 'The little patch nearest the kitchen window. Just try growing a few herbs for your first time.' But, despite her advice, I knew it was necessary to clear the whole plot. It is what William would have wanted, what he himself would have done.

All day I worked, inch by inch, edging down the full length of the plot, crouched on the lines of flat stepping stones that William had used to split the plot into sections to avoid compacting the ground. I'd read about compaction on the internet. I didn't mind the rain. I put my hood up and felt it brushing at my head. When I was little and the weather was bad, I'd make a den under the bay window on the avenue from a sheet draped between chairs dragged from the kitchen. I'd crawl in like a hibernating bear and listen to the rain slapping at the windows, curled around cushions taken from the sofa. I'd lie there reading until Mum's face appeared to say it was bath-time, or tea-time, or because Lucas was at the door and did I want to play.

I guide the blades of the scissors around the shape of my dad's head. It's intricate work. I feel like a surgeon. It needs to be done. A letter came from him today addressed to me. It used my real name. I didn't open it. I put it in the bin.

I don't remember much about the crash. I don't remember my arm breaking or anything like that. It's as though one of the doctors at the hospital took a pair of scissors and cut away a piece of my life, the part that began with me and Mum and Max in the car driving away from the house and ended with me in the hospital. In the gap in the middle are tiny floating fragments that don't make any sense.

Lucas came to see me in the hospital. He brought me a muffin wrapped neatly in a paper bag. He didn't know what to say. I didn't know either. I said, thank you for the muffin. I was glad he came but I didn't tell him that. Mum was there. I knew she'd been crying again and I didn't want her to think that I wasn't sad that Max wasn't alive any more. I didn't want her to see me writing notes and Lucas and I talking like Max and I used to do all the time. So we sat there looking in slightly different directions until it was time for Lucas to go.

Mum had arranged for one of her colleagues at the office, who had a trailer, to transport our belongings. Her colleague wasn't sure what to do with Max's things, so they ended up being taken along with everything else to the new flat that had been waiting for us. The day before Max's funeral, Mum unpacked the boxes. When I arrived at the flat for the first time, on the evening after the funeral, Max's room was there, full of his things where she had set them out, even his saxophone leaning against its stand next to the bed, like she was waiting for him to come back.

Dear Ms de Bruin,

I can't imagine for a moment that my sister would want the letter you say my father wrote for her, but I'd better ask her all the same. You know how families can be. If there's any more letters for me, feel free to bin them. My father is in a nursing home. They tell me he doesn't have long left, so he's not really going to be much use with your questions. One other thing. There was some unpleasantness at the house before he was admitted. Money was taken from his account by a carer, quite a lot. Her name is Irena Petrescu. The police know about her. If she makes contact at the house please let me know.

Regards,
Kevin Crosby

On the desk is a sheet of paper torn from one of Mum's sketch pads. On it I traced the shape of the kitchen garden. I'm basing my planting plan on the one William made in 1972. I know it was 1972 because he wrote the date in the top corner. I worked out that William's daughter was eleven that year. Tiny flowers have been pencilled in around the edges of the paper. I don't think William would have done that. The other plans I found, each one for a different year, don't have any flowers round the edges, so I think it must have been the eleven-year-old Rebecca who drew them. She and William must have sat here working out together where the carrots and potatoes and peas were to be planted in the vegetable plot that year, with Rebecca doodling her flowers round the edges as William, alongside her, pencilled in the names of the varieties they planned to sow.

It seems that William drew a plan at the start of every year. In each plan, the groups of vegetables are placed in different parts of the garden. I check with Google and discover that you are supposed to do this to avoid diseases in the vegetables and to help the soil to recover after it has spent a year helping one type of plant to grow. I fill in my plan, noting where I will plant things myself, with the brassicas in one quarter, potatoes and root vegetables next to them, beans and peas in front of the study window and salad leaves by the kitchen.

It's strange to think of William and the eleven-year-old Rebecca together at this desk organizing their planting. In the end, years later, when his daughter was a grown woman and they hadn't seen each other for a long time, William sat here in front of the typewriter trying to find the words to say to her in a letter. Instead of a letter, maybe he could have sent her a blank plan of the garden to fill in. Maybe she would have sent it back with tiny flowers drawn around the edges.

When I Google the name of the seed catalogue, I discover the company has a website where you can order your seeds online. I use the shopping basket on the site to pick out the seeds I need. When I can't find the kind that William grew that year, I choose another variety that sounds similar.

Lucas texted me:

Mouse, this is ridiculous. Just send me the name of the hotel. My mum says even if you have to move, most hotels will forward mail. Is it that you don't want me to write? Just say so if it is.

Lucas,

I would love you to write. You are my friend. But I need to tell you that we have moved again, and I don't think this new hotel could be relied on to safely pass on mail. The hotel we have moved to for another few days is a small family hotel in quite a grubby part of London. At least it was family run, but now there's only Mr Danczuk, who was pleased to see us but seems to have too much to do. I thought you might like to hear some details. Mr Danczuk is trying very hard not to be bald. He is short and has a big belly and a wheezy greyhound, which sleeps a lot in front of the electric fire in the small room behind the reception desk and which he takes for a walk twice a day.

The rooms on the floor above us are taken by a travelling circus, which apparently doesn't do any travelling or performing during the winter and which routinely spends its winter break at this hotel. I found this out from Mr Danczuk, whose wife and sister used to perform as part of the circus. As he explained, 'Who wants to sit in a leaky tent in a field in the middle of winter when you can stay at home and watch TV?'

I don't think Mr Danczuk likes the circus people very much. It's certainly true that they don't seem to talk much to the other guests. They just walk or cycle or stilt-walk right past them in the corridors, talking very fast to each other in some foreign language that doesn't sound like any other language I've ever heard, and they hang around the front step of the hotel smoking and looking sad. He complains that they never have enough money to pay for their rooms through the winter. Despite this, he seems to feel obliged to let the circus people come back to the hotel year after year.

From what I can tell, the circus hasn't been doing very well in recent years. Mr Danczuk says they should just close it down and have done with it, but they won't hear of it. They say it's in their blood, that the Circus Malmedy has existed since 1909, that their families have been circus performers for generations and that it is their duty to carry on. When they talk about these thing, Mr Danczuk says 'Shpah!', which I think means he doesn't agree, but he still lets them pay for their board by doing odd jobs around the hotel, which they do at all hours of the day and night. I think if you met Mr Danczuk, Lucas, you'd like him, even though he gets frustrated at the circus people and their antics on the top floor. I think his heart is in the right place. I think when I grow up I might like to join the Circus Malmedy. Lucas, will you come to watch me? I'll save a seat on the front row for you whenever you can come. Please don't be angry with me.

Yours sincerely,
Mouse

I check back through Mum's scores and notice something interesting. In the three weeks since we moved here, her average score is 0.8 higher than it was before we arrived. I think this is what is called statistically valid. I'm also fairly sure it's accurate because mostly I'm able to record Mum's scores once an hour. The only day when I have a problem keeping an accurate record is Thursday when I travel into the city for my session with Sadie, but I'm hopeful that this hasn't spoiled the research too much since I can usually estimate Mum's score from the tone of the texts she sends me while I'm in Manchester.

I begin to wonder if there are any other patterns I can find in the information about Mum that I have gathered in the Filofax. I tape together a series of blank sheets of paper in a long line that snakes off the edge of the desk at both sides and loops down onto the floor, then I draw a graph connecting all the scores together. My graph only goes back three months because, if I used all the numbers I had recorded, the piece of paper would stretch all the way through the kitchen and out into the walled vegetable garden. When I look at the curves of the graph throughout those three months, it occurs to me that Mum's score regularly dips part way through the morning and rises at lunchtime; then, at some point in the afternoon, it will dip again, only to rise back up in the early evening. Also, it drops quite low when something new happens, like when she has to drive somewhere new, or when someone comes from her office on welfare visits and she has to remember that she used to be a barrister.

I look out of the window. I think of the letters William wrote after the war, of the woman standing in her Austrian field with her horses asking 'Is this heaven?' I think of William as a young army officer smiling as he answers her. I wonder if this place Mum and I have arrived at might become heaven.

When I've filled up my online shopping basket with my purchases, I get Mum to come in to the study to type in her debit card details. She reads down the list of seeds I've ordered.

'Are we planning on feeding an army?' she says.

23

IRENA REACHES INTO the drawer holding the house-keeping money and deftly slides a ten pound note into the pocket of her jeans; William sees her do it. He catches sight of her naked on the landing after her shower; she senses he's there but lingers, combing injudicious strands of hair. It is a kind of dance they perform.

In the kitchen, she makes the sign of the cross. Not looking up, he says, 'You know, the Spanish Inquisition's holy men worked out how to tighten the noose in stages around a man's neck by using a stick.'

'What do you mean?' Irena says. 'A stick?'

'It allowed them to give a man just enough air to breathe, but his struggle for life would excite his excretory and sexual organs.'

'You think the only wicked things come from the Catholic church?'

William shrugs. 'Oliver Cromwell organized the killing of two thousand Irish in a day at Drogheda. King Leopold had the Belgians slaughter eight million in the Congo. He thought forced labour could bring civilization to the jungle. No, I don't regard wickedness as the preserve of the Catholic church.'

'Why do you say these things?' she asks curiously. 'You choose to upset me?'

'You would choose not to know?'

'I don't want to know; no, thank you.' And she goes about her business, which is tending to his care now that William is home from the hospital after his stroke.

On her third day, Irena had told him her story. By the weekend he had offered her a room. Privacy was hardly a problem now that he was mostly in a wheelchair and could no longer get upstairs. He didn't believe the decision was made out of loneliness. He felt sure it was no more than good sense, maybe laced with some small thread of charity.

He had made one thing clear to the social worker at the hospital. He would not move into a nursing home. He would see out his remaining months at the farm. His bed had been brought down to the sitting room. A ramp was fitted to the kitchen door so he could get in and out of the house. A supply of frozen meals was delivered once a week. There was talk of a downstairs shower being installed. He told them there was no family to be contacted. As a result, the financial assessment wasn't carried out until he was back home. It turned out that the savings he held in the bank took him over the threshold, which meant he had to pay for the hour's care commissioned by social services at either end of the day. It made sense to him, therefore, to barter extra hours from Irena in exchange for a bedroom and a bath that were no use to him any more. In return for the room, they agreed that she would be available if he needed help fetching and carrying, emptying the commode. She would do his shopping and run other errands over and above the work the agency paid her to do for him. When she went out on her other calls for the agency she would carry a mobile that he could ring her on if he fell or was in distress. The arrangement was against the agency's rules, so they told no one.

Irena was the fourth worker sent by the agency; the last one. By then, word had spread among the local women employed by the agency who, as a result, were reluctant to be reproached twice a day by some embittered former teacher still clinging to the authority the classroom had once given him to humiliate. Irena, the outsider, the employee from Poland who had only recently been employed by the agency, was his last chance.

Before the stroke, sleep had not come easily to him. He was careful not to drink more than one glass of wine. If he did, then after two or three hours in bed he would be wide awake for the rest of the night. It puzzles him that now he can routinely nod off without any warning sense of fatigue.

He has movement down one side. Enough to propel the wheelchair, to feed, to shave. Enough to get himself from the bed to the chair and back. His speech had started to return within a few days of the stroke, though if he is tired he feels as if he has to chew a word and spit it out. A decision was taken at the hospital that further physiotherapy wouldn't help much. In defiance, he practises walking each day. Three laps of the kitchen: the eyes of a puff adder, the frame of a heron. It exhausts him. Irena holds him steady. He will not give way. For the same reason, he will not take the Prozac he has been prescribed. Each day, Irena puts it out for him with the bagful of other gaily coloured pills; each day, William leaves it on the side, like a piece of unwanted gristle. He would rather stare his demons down. He has managed to stop the dribbling that distressed him in the hospital. Unforgivably, no one else in there seemed to mind. He can eat real food again, though it tastes of nothing. In the hospital, he was confined to meals that gathered in puddles in the dishes they placed in front of him, and to endless vitamin drinks, which he is still required to take twice a day. At least he doesn't need the straws any more. In over eighty years it never occurred to him that it might be possible to feel gratitude for such a thing. He sometimes has an urge to reach out for his younger self crouching there in the Italian mud, shake him and, out of spite, tell him about the fucking straws.

He sits there half the morning by the window, not saying anything. What to do? What to do? Some small resolve inside him eventually breaks, like a levee giving way to rising water. She sees him crying, the tears squeezed out silently from this parched and ridiculous old man.

'Sshh,' she says, soft as a lullaby at the edge of the room.

'Fuck off,' he stabs at her. He stares out of the window. He cannot turn to her. He cannot bear himself. 'I shat myself,' he says. 'It's everywhere.'

'SShh,' she whispers again, drifting a few steps closer, enough to signal that she is not repelled. 'I get you cleaned up.'

She cleans him as he leans against the bed, wiping carefully each flap and buckle of skin between his legs, his scrotum, penis, the narrow hips. She helps him dress, takes care of the soiled clothing, the sheets, disinfects the chair. He says nothing. She makes tea. He takes the cup from her. He will not look her in the eye. He cannot measure how much he is reduced, how many things are shattered, how far is left to fall. The clock on the mantelpiece ticks.

After a while, she speaks into the silence between them.

'We came in a lorry,' she says. 'There were two children – a boy, a girl. Not mine. At the border, before the tunnel, we have to go into a small box in the back of the lorry to get through the customs.'

He makes a hesitant cross-examination. 'But anyone from Poland can come here to work.'

'Not Poland.'

'Where?'

'Albania.'

It dawns on him what it is she is telling him.

'A man in our town, he is allowed to stay here, in UK. A lawyer agreed *indefinite leave* with the courts. Marco. He says this. He brings his wife over. After this they bring children over. Not his children. Children of other people in the town. They make money for him, stealing. His wife, she gets money from the state for them also. Benefits, yes? Money? She claims the children belong to her. Many of them come. Marco sends the money back to his brother. In the town, Marco and his brother have big houses, marble floors. Mansions. Big cars. Marco is a big man in the town. They ask me to come over since I speak English. They need me to help them. His wife goes always back and forward to Albania. It's a chance for me to go to England. The only chance. Marco says he likes me; he trusts me. He says he can get me papers in the end to say I am from Poland. To stay in England for good, to work. In that way, I can go to college finally after the work, after Marco is done and goes back to Albania. Then, he says, I can choose what to do. He gets me fake documents from the lawyer saying I have leave to remain in UK. I must look after the business. Fill in forms and documents. Make claims. Send money transfers back. So I come to England. He says this is a chance for me. He says I should be grateful. You understand how grateful I need to be to Marco? Very grateful. I have to show him. I wait and wait. What else to do? After one year he gets me documents saying "indefinite leave" from the lawyer so I can claim benefits and work, to give some more money to Marco. Another thing to be grateful for. You know what I am saying. But as soon as I get the document, I go in the night.'

'Where is Marco now?' he asks.

'London. He came looking for me one month ago. I have a cousin in Manchester and he came to her. I can't go there any more. Is not safe for her. So I tell people always I am Polish in case he comes looking again for me. In case he asks questions about a stupid Albanian woman he has come looking for, telling that I stole from him.'

Irena sips her tea. 'Stupid. Stupid.'

The two of them stare out of the window.

'I think, maybe,' she says. 'I think sometimes are worse things to do than to have your bottom cleaned. I think this. That is all.'

That was how William came to offer her the room.

24

MARY SLIPS INTO THE ROOM. She takes her place in a vacant chair, gathers herself, half smiles in case anyone is looking at her, glances down. She realizes that she is holding her breath. The eight chairs form a circle at one end of the too-big hall. There are markings on the floor for a badminton court and overlapping designs for children's ball games. It occurs to her that the Kelly brothers might come here on youth club nights. She wonders if they let off firecrackers in the corridor; whether they carve obscenities into the community centre's ornate plasterwork. She exhales slowly.

When they begin, the tutor introduces her to the other members of the writing group. The tutor is dressed in layers. Her elegant hands move in rhythm with her words. She is dark eyed, bone thin. Mary wonders if she should have worn a better jumper.

One by one the women in the group – there are no men – read out the pieces they have written in the week since they last met. The tutor listens attentively. She praises each piece with equal enthusiasm. She talks about point of view and character and structure. The women listen, intent on absorbing the insights that will enable their own doughy prose to rise, take flight and soar. And Mary, eyes narrowed, observing a piece of the floor in the centre of the circle formed by the women's shoes, is carried back to the cusp of adulthood, to the summer when, as Mary Challener, she walked up the hill twice a week to William Crosby's farm in preparation for her Oxbridge examination.

'I can teach you how to pass the examination,' William Crosby had said to the seventeen-year-old Mary, 'or I can teach you how to think for yourself. It's your money. It makes no difference to me.'

It wasn't her money, though, it was her mother's money, garnered from three evenings a week spent on a production line assembling parts for televisions once her day job in a short-order printer's was done. Mary recognized what William was doing. He was extending an invitation into a different kind of adult life.

'Teach me to think,' she had said, more boldly than she'd intended. She'd expected him to smile. That's what the boys in the town would have done. But he didn't smile.

'All right,' he said, 'so tell me everything you know. We'll start from there.'

And so she spread out before him all the scraps of wisdom she had gathered in a life, the furthest extremities of which were marked by Blackpool beach and Wigan Casino, and a library copy of *The Female Eunuch*. When she was done, he dismissed it all piece by piece, like a border guard riffling through the contents of a handbag whose accumulated trifles he was discarding one by one in search of valuables. He ran his hands along the shelves of books in his study. She watched him pluck down half a dozen one after another. He passed them to her. He told her to go away and read them, and then come back on Tuesday.

'Do you want me to write an essay or something, Mr Crosby?' she asked.

He waved a hand. 'William,' he said. 'No essay. Just come back and tell me what you *felt*.'

She'd walked back down the hill, clutching William Crosby's books. She knew that a door was opening quietly into a different world. She felt restless. She was full of possibilities.

◆◆◆

What put a stop to those possibilities were the boys; first Anthony, then Luke. And this became her life. This fact. *They* became her life.

She was the same person, but her life grew heavier to carry. The person she might have become narrowed. She was a woman with two sons, one with a learning disability and one whose slow fall into drug use had led to a hazy diagnosis of schizophrenia. She needed to feed them, clothe them, protect them from injustice, give them life and hope despite themselves. They had none of their own, so she gave them hers.

It was strange and unexpected for her path and William Crosby's to cross again after all those years. It didn't feel like anything remarkable – that is, if someone nailing a sheep's heart to your door can be unremarkable. It didn't seem to augur anything very much. But it reminded her of the person she had once been. Of the promise. Of the girl walking down the hill from the Crosbys' farmhouse with an armful of books and a restlessness inside her. That flare of memory was the impulse which led her to put her name down for the writing group when she discovered there was one running in a community centre in the town.

Before the session ends, the tutor sets the group their homework for the week. She asks them to write about 'a chance encounter'. This will be their theme for the week. She encourages them to use any approach, any style they like. She reminds them of some of the technical aspects they have talked about during the session, of point of view and character. She makes writing sound like a recipe for baking cakes. Mary wants to raise her voice and say that this isn't how writing is. It's not a recipe to be followed. But she stays silent.

25

PING PING.

My mobile receives a text just as I'm lifting the Dauphinoise potatoes out of the stove and onto the table. I think I put too much garlic in, and not enough cream. It's crisped up nicely on the surface, but, when I prise back the top layer, the potatoes underneath seem to have toughened into the texture of drying clay.

I check the message.

On the internet I read about someone who invented a forgiveness machine.

The message is from 266 – the texter whose number ends in 266 and who is still exchanging messages with me several weeks after I received the first one as I was sitting on the Metro the day I dodged Lucas in Piccadilly Gardens. I get a new text from 266 every few days.

Do you ever get really frightened of something? I texted back that first time, as the tram slipped out of the city.

What, you want a list? 266 replied, which I kind of liked.

I think about the forgiveness machine. I text back, *How does it work?* I go to find Mum to let her know tea is ready. While I'm serving, my phone pings again. Mum sits down. I pass her a plate with the Dauphinoise and some garden peas I warmed. I read the reply.

You write down what you want to forgive, or what you need forgiving for. You feed the paper into the machine and it sucks it through a set of tubes. At the far end of the machine, it shreds the piece of paper. It's on show at an arts centre in California.

I watch Mum do her best to chew her way through the Dauphinoise. She smiles at me when I look across the table. I score her a 3.9. I get slightly concerned at the waft of garlic in each dense, dry mouthful.

After supper I send another text to 266.

Do you think it's okay to talk to dead people?

Dear Lucas,

I discovered that Mr Danczuk and some of the circus performers play poker late at night down in the basement of our hotel. I wrote, *Don't you ever go to sleep?* and showed it to Mr Danczuk. He told me he hasn't slept much since the day his wife and her sister died performing their high-wire act for Circus Malmedy in a small town near Antwerp, which is in Belgium. I think that's partly why he lets the circus people keep coming back to his hotel year after year. They keep him company at night playing poker when everyone else is asleep.

I'm spending a lot of time at the moment with Velma, who's a trapeze artiste with the circus. She is teaching me to stilt-walk. I can hear her starting to practise on the floor above our room now so I'd better go.

Ciao (that's Italian),
Mouse

The text from Lucas says: *I don't believe you're living in a hotel, Mouse. I don't believe any of the stories about the stupid hotels. If they're true, text me the name of the hotel right now or I'm done trying to be your friend.*

I need to work out what to do about Lucas. But first I have bigger fish to fry.

I tell Sadie about Mum's scores. I unfurl the graph I made so that it stretches across the floor of her office. I explain on the whiteboard about the graph points, and the line that sways up and down as it connects the three months of scores. Sadie agrees that my approach is very thorough. She says it's a comprehensive piece of research. I explain about the patterns I think I can detect in the lines on the graph.

We take a break for Sadie to make a brew. She always brings me an orange squash, or hot chocolate if it's a cold day outside. Then she suggests that she needs to do some research of her own. 'I know you'll appreciate the importance of collecting raw data,' she says. She explains that the best way to collect the information from me in a statistically valid way is to conduct the research using the 'Yes/No' model, which was developed at Harvard University.

By speech therapists? I write.

'*For* speech therapists,' Sadie says. 'For people like me, to help the clients we work with.'

I only have to say yes or no, she tells me. No deviating, or that will invalidate the research. 'Is that okay?' she asks.

I guess so.

Sadie prints out 'Yes' and 'No' on two pieces of card and passes them to me.

'You have to hold one of them in each hand,' she says. She takes a slurp of her tea and says, 'Ready?'

I haven't heard of the Yes/No model, but I realize that if it's been developed by Harvard University then it must be a statistically valid one.

I nod. Sadie smiles, gesturing at my hands. I remember the pieces of card. I hold up the Yes card.

'Okay, here we go. First question. Do you have any speech?'

I hold up the No card.

'Was there a time when you did have speech?' Yes.

'Do you want to speak?' Yes.

'Do you currently live with other people?' Yes.

'Do any of them have difficulty speaking?' No.

'Do you associate any major life events with your loss of speech?' No.

'Do you have any other symptoms or illnesses?' No.

'How content or satisfied are you? Very?' No.

'Moderately?' No.

'Just a little?' Yes.

'What about the person or people living with you. So, your mum. Very content?' No.

'Moderately?' No.

'Just a little?' No.

'Does she know she is unhappy?' Yes.

'Is your mum poorly?'

I look at the two cards, hesitating.

'Could she be unhappy because she is poorly?' No.

'She is not poorly, she's unhappy?' Yes.

'Did something *make* her unhappy?' Yes.

'Did that thing make you unhappy, too?' Yes.

'But not as unhappy as it made your mum?' No.

'Will she become happy?' Yes.

'Will that happen soon?' No.

'Are there things you can do to help?' Yes.

'Does it help her that you make things for her? Bake cakes. Cook for her?' Yes.

'But it might take a long time for these lots of little things to make her happy again?' Yes.

'Is that okay? That it might take a long time for your mum to get better – sorry, to feel happy?' Yes.

'Because you love her?' Yes.

'Will it help her when you go back to school?' No.

'Because she'll be on her own during the day?' Yes.

'But she wants you to go back to school?'

'...'

'You need to answer for this to work, Mouse.'

I lean across to the whiteboard. *She says she wants me to go to school.*

'She says she wants you to go?' Yes.

'But you think she really wants you to stay with her?' Yes.

'For now?' Yes.

'For a while?' Yes.

'Maybe for a long while?' Yes.

'Does she get lonely at the farmhouse?' No.

'Is that because you're there with her?' Yes.

'Do you get lonely there?' No.

'Do people come and visit you there?' No.

'Do any of your friends come and visit?' No.

'Does Lucas visit you at home?'

'...'

'Does Lucas visit, Mouse?' No.

Sadie nods, as if I've done something good by telling her Lucas doesn't come to visit me at the farmhouse, but she doesn't say anything.

'Would he like to come?' Yes.

'Can you tell me why he doesn't come?' No.

'Will you be able to tell me one day why not?' Yes.

'But not now?' No.

'What about your mum – does anyone come to see your mum?' Yes.

'Often?' No.

'The people at work? Does someone from her firm come?' Yes.

'Just now and then?' Yes.

'Does that seem to help? When someone visits from work? Do your mum's scores go up afterwards?' No.

'Do you think your mum prefers it when it's just the two of you?' Yes.

'That must make you feel quite responsible for her?' Yes.

'Mouse, do you know what single thing would make your mum most happy?'

I sit and think for a moment. As I am thinking, it occurs to me that this – the questions from Sadie, the yeses and noes, the need to be honest in each of my responses so that the research won't be invalidated – is like taking a lie detector test. There aren't any wires attached to me to measure my physical reactions, which is what happens with a real lie detector test, but when people know that you have to tell the truth in order for the research to be statistically valid, you don't need the wires. You only need to ask your questions, and it works the same way.

I hold up the 'Yes' card.

'Would it be okay for you to write it on the board?' Sadie says. 'To save me keep asking, like, a hundred yes or no questions.'

So I write on the whiteboard.

For Max still to be alive.

'But that isn't going to happen, is it?' No.

'That must be hard for your mum?' Yes.

'To lose Max, like that, when she was driving the car?' Yes.

'And hard for you?' Yes.

'In some ways, maybe, even harder for you than for your mum?' No.

'Your mum's older than you. Shouldn't she be better at dealing with it than you?' No.

'Are you better at dealing with it than her?' Yes.

'It sounds like she relies on you a lot?' Yes.

'And she loves you, your mum?' Yes.

'She loved Max, too?' Yes.

'But Max isn't around any more. Max died on the night of the car crash?' Yes.

'What would have happened if it had been you who died that night, Mouse, and Max who was left? Would Max have looked after your mum?' Yes.

'And would it have been just as bad for your mum, to lose you rather than Max?'

'…'

'Mouse, do you think your mum loved Max more than you?'

'...'

'Mouse?' No.

And I wonder, as I hold up the card and Sadie makes her note on the pad, whether she can hear what I can hear, which is the quiet alarm of the lie detector machine going *beep beep beep* inside my head.

26

My dear girl,

She was all I could think about. In the chaos and madness that is the circus of the end of war, in that heaving, stinking swarm of people and animals, shit and decay, drunkenness and giddy optimism, what I thought about as I woke each day was Anna.

The morning after my tour of the camp, I went to find her. My excuse was that I wanted to appoint her formally (on behalf of the British government, you understand) as my interpreter, as someone who could escort me round the camp, translating for me, and help me deal with the Cossacks in my lowly role as liaison officer. The truth was that the English could no more police the encampment than we could turn the fast-flowing waters of the River Drau into wine. We could hardly wire the perimeter of a camp that stretched for twelve miles between Lienz at one end of the valley and Oberdrauburg at the other. We were entirely dependent on the Cossacks policing themselves. My plan was simple. I would tell Anna what needed to be done, starting with persuading thirty thousand Cossacks not to shit in the river but to construct latrines. She would communicate this to General Domanov and his staff, who were based at a hotel across town from the one commandeered by Colonel Malcolm for the Argyles. Then, armed with their approval, she and I would make a tour of the settlement by jeep once a day to ensure that everything was in order, with Anna helping to convey the orders as we went.

I found her that morning in the barracks at Peggetz, a mile down the valley from Lienz. She was conducting an English lesson for children, many of whom, along with the women, had been housed there. The barracks made a mockery of the notion that this was a Cossack 'army'. It was, in truth, little more than a refugee camp. People of every shape and size passed through the corridor that Anna was using as a classroom. I stood at the back and marvelled at her, a woman in a girl's body, unperturbed, sleeves rolled up, hair chopped short, eyes shining, changing the world for the better in infinitesimally small and patient stages as passers-by shuffled to and from the overcrowded canteen.

Eventually, she caught sight of me. She set the children to copying the set of English words she had been writing up on the wall in chalk and came across to me.

'Captain Crosby, always when I look I find you there watching.'

I affected a small bow of my head to reacquaint myself with her. She asked if I had enjoyed the tour of the camp the previous night. I told her that I had, and set out my plans for her.

'I am to ask you to take up the role on a formal basis from eight o'clock in the morning. There is some urgency as the Red Cross are expected to arrive at the camp any day.'

She shrugged. 'I have work here,' she said, 'and I need to help the colonel. I gave my word to my father that I would.'

'This is more important,' I told her grandly.

She ignored my rudeness. 'More important than teaching these little ones?'

'I think so, yes.'

'What makes you think I will do this?' she asked, tilting her head as if to test the remark.

In the army, one gets accustomed to passing information either to those above you in rank or to those below you. Momentarily, I think, I confused her reluctance with the obduracy of a corporal.

'Field Marshal Alexander is asking you to help the Allied

cause,' I told her, foolishly.

She looked me in the eye, the way a corporal would not. 'You met him personally for this?' she asked.

'Of course not, no. Not, personally.' I realized I had overreached.

'Perhaps, Captain, when you next have afternoon tea with the field marshal to discuss my critical role in the war, which by the way is over, you could remind him please to finally reply to our letters requesting him to confirm that we are to be settled in the West.'

I took a breath. 'What I should have said... what I meant was that you can assume that any request from me has the authority of a chain of command that rises to the top.'

'All the way to Field Marshal Alexander, who takes his afternoon tea with you?'

'I never said I had tea with Alexander.'

'You are a funny man, Captain William Crosby. So proper. So deliberate.'

'It's my job, I'm a soldier.'

She shook her head. 'No, it's more than that.' She laughed. 'I think I made you blush.'

Behind her, some of the children were growing restive. She glanced round. 'I need to go back to them,' she said, 'before there is disorder. You will understand disorder, I think, being a soldier.'

'What about the request?' I asked.

'From Field Marshal Alexander?'

'From the British army.'

'What about you, Captain Crosby? What do you want?' And she looked at me in a way I believe no one had looked at me before, as if I might have been both everything and nothing to her.

'I want you to help me,' I said.

'You see,' she said, turning away towards the children, 'that wasn't so hard, was it?'

At eight the next morning, Anna presented herself at the

reception of the hotel designated as the British HQ in Lienz. I arrived twenty minutes later from my own billet further up the hill and, from the off, was somehow always half a step behind her. Any notion of rank, or of me being the officer in charge, had been dispelled the day before. Instead, there was a kind of understanding between us that she (representing the Cossacks stranded as refugees in an Austrian valley) and I (representing the victorious British army) would collaborate in working towards a decent end. We would, between us, prove that the tide of war, launched after all to defend the integrity of small nations, had been worth unleashing and would wash away to leave a permanent Cossack enclave settled somewhere in the debris of middle Europe.

I had the strangest sense of timelessness travelling round the valley each day. It was accentuated, I suppose, by the ending of hostilities, the gradual subsiding of the reflex that sets men close to the front line on an almost permanent alert, and the fact that each night gave way to another flawless early summer's morning. Somehow every new day in this golden place seemed to last a month.

When the Red Cross arrived and we showed them round they were, as I had been, taken aback at what they found in what purported to be a refugee camp. Churches, a functioning community, a school, a choir, all established by the Cossacks themselves, were flourishing. There were even advanced plans for a Cossack newspaper to be published in the valley. A passing stranger might have assumed the community had been long settled here rather than arriving only two weeks before, having dragged their wagons and cattle, their horses and camels, with them over the Plöckenpass.

Already, I think, the Cossacks were reconciled to the reality that it might be many months, or even years, before the rights of settlement to new lands in the West were painstakingly negotiated by the Allies and, if necessary, agreed with the representatives of the defeated powers. But more than this, I think they were anxious to demonstrate that they were a fledgling nation which was capable of managing its own affairs. And so, as they waited patiently for Field Marshal Alexander to reply to the entreaties made on their behalf, they settled down to living their lives in the valley that was theirs for now.

It was in this nation of fields, of tents, wooden carts and animals, through which I began my daily round, accompanied by Anna and the boy, who refused to leave her side. The three of us became a confederacy of our own moving about the camp; Anna driving Vasilenko's Fiat as she liked to do, happily slamming the beast of a car into gear, me beside her watching (paternally, I liked to think) over my twelve miles of encampments, the boy in the back seat, sometimes watching, sometimes sleeping, never speaking – the result, I learned, of unspoken events in that period of the war when the rest of his family had died.

As we made our daily tour we checked that supplies were being distributed adequately across the camp. We did what we could about the sanitation problem, encouraging people to dig out functioning latrines. We let people know about medical facilities, about food deliveries, about the school. We scotched unfounded rumours that seemed to spring up from nowhere among such huge numbers of people about outbreaks of disease (always somewhere else, unspecified), or groups of Azerbaijanis or Georgians under Allied control elsewhere in Austria being handed over to the Red Army, or of local bandits rustling Cossack cattle.

I say 'we', but in truth it was Anna who spoke to the people, calmed their fears, scolded them for their disrespect towards Great Britain for believing rumours, told them to be patient. Then she reported back to me, and left me to accept the praise of my superiors at Lienz HQ for maintaining order and calm across the camp.

I learned every morning to pack my pockets with sweets and chocolates, ready for the children who surrounded us and clamoured for them whenever we stepped out of

Vasilenko's car. I set Brody to the task of rounding up enough supplies of sweets from our men's rations to help me meet the demand from the Cossack children. He seemed eager enough to help and mocked me gleefully over the 'family' I had overnight adopted and the news, which he thought hilarious, that Anna had started teaching me to ride. I ignored his jibes. Yet the truth was that my previous life in northern England now began to seem as remote as the prospect of my once having been a Japanese samurai, or a medieval carpenter.

27

THE NEWSPAPERS STACKED IN PILES in the hall mean the door will not open more than a few inches before it jams. Joseph Brody's technique for getting in and out of his flat is to straddle his way around the door, gripping his stick under one arm, being careful not to bend too far or put too much weight on either knee at any one time. He is a big man. In his youth it was a blessing, but now his frame is collapsing. Each day is a roll call for which parts of him are working and which are not. Coming and going is a complex business.

Rhona liked to keep things. That was part of the reason she had been admitted to the hospital. She and Joseph met when she moved on from the hospital to Hamilton House. She told him that collecting took the difficult edge off her days. At Hamilton House she was acquiring teapots and glass owls. She didn't tell the staff, worried that they wouldn't understand. When, eventually, the two of them moved into a flat together, he tolerated her need to collect things. He towered above her, protecting her. He wanted to take the difficult edge off her days. Only once, shortly after they moved into their small flat, did he object to her need to save. He said they didn't need to keep so many of the tinfoil plates and dishes left over from their supermarket meals that she had washed and stored away. They had a row during which she pleaded. Joseph hadn't heard her voice assert itself before. In the six months at Hamilton House she had talked in whispers. The argument finished with Joseph taking two bin bags full of the damned things from the back of the pantry and throwing them down the waste chute used by all the tenants in their high-rise block. The following night he woke and saw she was gone from the bed. He found her in the basement, sat in the cage amid a week's worth of rubbish, sifting for the foil plates, tears staining her pale and wondrous face, and he vowed never to do such a thing again.

Steadily they filled the pantry, the surfaces of the bedroom, the corners of the living room, the kitchen. Things edged out into a no-man's land, encroaching on their human space. In the end, Joseph put chalk marks on the lino floors so they could navigate between their four rooms along narrowing gangways. He began to keep back newspaper articles, carrier bags. Useful things. He kept visitors away. He took care to meet his daughter away from the flat. He didn't want her seeing it. He didn't want Rhona to be judged after all that she had survived. He didn't want her misunderstood.

When Rhona died, he found this need to retain possessions had passed from her to him as if it were a living thing he had to take care of. He tried to make a fresh start, to throw things out, but they were hers. He would sit for hours with a glass owl in his hand wondering whether to put it in the bin, to start clearing the decks. He would hold a dress of hers in his hand and always, in the end, he would put it back again. By saving things, he was saving part of her. And gradually he began to accrue items of his own that other people might have thrown away once their useful lives were over: toothbrushes; jam jars; light bulbs; worn-out socks. They gathered around him like sediment.

Joseph sits in the café that looks onto the bay. In their eleven years together he and Rhona came any number of times a year, caught the bus from the city, sat in this café, watched the roll of the waves, spent pennies in the amusement arcade, ate candy floss, paddled at the edge of the grey Scottish sea with their shoes and socks gripped in their hands. Somewhere in the flat is a boxful of salt cellars that Rhona collected from here one visit at a time. It wasn't theft, it was harvesting. It was a way of preserving the goodness of the day. It was a protection against what else lay out there. Christian priests, Joseph Brody knows, had done no less for two thousand years with the bones of saints.

He writes a letter. Steam drifts from his cup of tea. Drizzle pricks the foggy window. The café is dense with warmth. There are no other customers. Now and then he looks out into the bay. A couple in overcoats are braving the beach, her arm in his. A dog-walker with her headscarf bent into the wind throws something for a Jack Russell and a heavy Labrador, who bound after it with disproportionate energy. The chimes of the smaller dog's bark are the only noises that carry to him above the insistent whispers of the sea. His head turns back to the page. He takes sips of his tea. He picks up the salt cellar on the table, feels its indentations between his fingers. He lays it down again. The weather is closing in. The edges of the bay merge into the mist. The couple have left the beach. Only the woman with the two dogs remains.

'I came to see you in Milan,' he writes. 'You were asleep. You slept for days. I wanted to wake you and thank you. You know what for. But I did not. I left you sleeping. You deserved nothing less. Those few moments when it is actually possible to speak the truth pass us by and are lost. I let you sleep. You never knew I came. This is my thank you now. I have saved it for the end.'

He looks up. The woman with her dogs has gone. The beach is deserted. Joseph folds the letter, slips it inside the envelope that is addressed to William Crosby, fixes the stamp he lifts from his wallet. He takes one final sip of tea, feels its sweetness run over his teeth. He stands and buttons his coat.

'Thank you,' he says into the silence of the room. The man behind the counter glances up from his paper.

Joseph steps out of the café, holding the envelope in one hand. A car whips by close to the pavement and he watches it pass and swiftly disappear down the road. Then quiet descends on the bay once more.

28

EARLY MORNING. THE AIR is kind of soupy. The trees hang still. I walk across the yard holding a small clutch of letters, and a parcel that fits under my arm. The *craik craik* of a single crow breaks into the silence. Only if you go up close to the brushwork of trees can you see the swells of buds beginning to appear.

I watched the postman's van drive up the lane. I was waiting for him. One of the letters he delivered has a cellophane window and a council postmark. Most likely it's from the education department. Another one was from Mum's chambers, most likely asking if she's ready to go back to work. There was one from the supervised contact people and one addressed to me in my dad's handwriting. I placed two circulars and the gas bill on the doormat for Mum to find and brought the others outside with me.

I rest the letters on the lid of the oil drum and shake the parcel gently. There is a satisfying shuffle from the contents. I put the parcel down on the floor and lift the lid from the oil drum. I open the envelopes in turn, loosely scrunching the pages inside one by one and then the envelopes and letting them fall down into the drum. I pull William's old lighter out of my coat pocket and use it to kindle a flame at the edge of the final envelope. I let it fall. The lick of flame spreads at the base of the drum. I slide the lid on top of the drum. I pick up my parcel and walk away, around the house, into the walled garden.

I stand there, curious.

I have a sense that something is out of place.

I look at the dark, even soil of the vegetable plot. It takes a moment to work out what it is.

William's footprints are in the earth.

I walk across and stand over them, looking down, not frightened. Curious. Puzzled. In a steady line beside the imprint of his boots the early broad bean seeds have sprouted. They are straining up into the promise of a new growing season. I press my hand into the shape of one of William's footprints. I feel the rim of his sole with my fingertips to persuade myself they are real. I trace the crescents and indents of the tread. Somehow I find it reassuring. How else would the world be organized? Perhaps, it occurs to me, it is simply the case that you can live somewhere so long, feel the need to be there so much, that you can dream yourself back there.

And then, out of the corner of my eye, I'm suddenly aware of a movement. There's a flash of dull red at the edge of the open gate leading out to the paddock. Something alert but focused on itself. A hot black nose edging at the ground. Sharp ears cocked.

'Fox.'

He seems unreal, but the thin pant of his breath shows that he's a solid animal. A real fox. Perfect in his russet colours. A perfect fox. The shock is not the fox, but that I'm not alone. I've grown accustomed to being the only moving creature on the land. The postman and the supermarket van make their deliveries and scurry down the track again. Mum stays mostly in the house. The birds don't count. They are creatures of the air, not grounded, not belonging here. This is my land; mine and William's. And yet, here is a fox. I hold still, rooted to my spot. We stand here, the fox and I, sharing the land between us. Then his head shifts slightly and he catches sight of me. He seems to examine me in the way I found myself examining William's footstep – like I'm an imposition, something straying into a landscape that is his. His stare says that I won't outlast him here. He refuses to yield. He holds and holds. My breath is gathered up inside me. And then, as if I dreamed him up, he blinks and turns and is gone.

I resist the urge to run to the open gate. I stay where I'm standing and let him move away at his own pace. And only when the moment has passed, when he has been swallowed by the land and I'm alone again with my thoughts, does it occur to me that the word came out of mouth.

Dear Ms de Bruin,

You wrote to Joseph Brody. He was my father. The people living at his old address forwarded your letter. I suppose you couldn't know. My father died several years ago. I did write to tell William Crosby, but he didn't come to the funeral. He wasn't the only one, I suppose. I'm afraid even my sister didn't go. I guess people don't know how to react. It's not like dying of cancer or being in a hit and run, is it? Still, I figured that, whatever happened, he was still my father. I used to drive across once a month and meet him somewhere or other for lunch. He would tell me that things were fine. You could see they weren't. That's how I remember him in his later years; a big man bending improbably into cramped little spaces in cafés and smiling meekly for me. But he wouldn't ever come to us. He was never quite the same after my mother left him. I never saw his flat until after he died. When I did, I thought: how did my father end up like this? But, of course, he didn't end up like that, did he? He walked into the sea one winter's day in his coat and they found his body washed up the next morning five miles down the coast with stones in his pockets and a salt cellar gripped in his right hand. That's how he ended up. My sister told me that she thinks suicide is an angry thing. But I don't think my father was angry. I think he was mostly tired.

When we finally cleared the flat and got rid of the

> rubbish there was a box of items left over that I kept. Things he'd saved from the war. I thought you might find one or two of them useful where they mention your man William Crosby, or where he is in the photograph with my father. They're no good to me any more. I feel like I've sucked what goodness I can from them. So I'm sending them on to you. And, anyway, I've been through it all a hundred times and none of it has been able to tell me what he was thinking when he walked into the sea that day. You ask your William Crosby if he knows the answer to that one. I don't suppose he does. These things become history so quickly and get forgotten, don't you think?
>
> Yours sincerely,
> Ailsa Thorpe

I have been emailing nursing homes in the city. If you Google it, the computer tells you that there are hundreds of nursing homes and care homes across the ten boroughs of Greater Manchester. That's before you start counting the ones just over the border in Lancashire. When I started to research them, I needed to explain to Mum that I was spending so much time on the computer because I was working on an assignment. It was a useful thing to say because I need her to think that home education is something we should give serious thought to extending after the summer, especially if we decide to stay here.

I've been emailing a dozen homes a day, asking each of them in turn if they have a William Crosby on their books. The first reply that came back said

> Miss de Bruin, we have no resident by the name of William Crosby on our books here at Elham Grove. Best wishes,
>
> Priti Viswanath

Dear Lucas,

We're on the move again. I'm very much looking forward to a time when we are more settled and you really will be able to visit us. For now, let me tell you that the circus people came to blows arguing over their debts. I think the fight was the final straw for Mr Danczuk, who demanded that everybody from the circus should leave his hotel.

Mum protested, but with no success. And since the remnants of Circus Malmedy have been forced to leave the hotel, Mum felt obliged that we should leave as well. That's why we have moved with the circus folk into a small boarding house at the end of a dark alley. Mum is paying for two rooms there, with five of the circus people sleeping in one room, with Mum taking the bed, and Velma sharing the adjacent room with me. The walls are thin. At night I can hear some of the circus folk in Mum's room snoring. Lucas, I know you haven't texted me in a while but I will keep you informed as I know you will be worried.

Yours,
Mouse

I unlock the door to the outhouse and go inside. I place my parcel on the workbench and open it up. It's a hand-held, battery-powered vacuum cleaner I bought using Mum's credit card. The contents of the package that arrived a few days ago are already spread out on the workbench – lengths of transparent plastic tubing, a hamster exercise ball and a set of plastic 'Y' joints. I start a list of the other things I now need: screwdriver; pliers; tape; shredder.

I followed the link that 266 texted me and downloaded a photograph of the machine in America. As 266 said, it looks mostly like an elaborate hamster run. The plastic tubing is connected at one end to a suction device. It separates into two lines, comes back in the middle and then loops in a couple of neat swirls before it connects at the other end to the paper shredder.

I researched some more on the internet about the woman who made it. She lived with a writer. He wrote brilliant, complicated books. He was on a lot of medication. He suffered panic attacks, which is what happens sometimes with Mum. Quite a lot of things about the world made the writer nervous, which surprises me. I didn't think writers would be so afraid of things. It makes me think that maybe I could be a writer. The man who was a famous writer wrote in his garage. He didn't go outside much. He felt safer that way. When he died, his partner built a forgiveness machine. I made a note in my Filofax to read books by David Foster Wallace. I wrote a letter to his partner. I sent it to the Pasadena Art Center, California, where her invention had been displayed.

> Dear Karen Green
>
> I wanted to ask you if your forgiveness machine worked. I'm thinking of making one.
>
> Yours faithfully,
> Mouse de Bruin

I unfold the photograph I downloaded and printed. To one side of the outhouse window is a cork noticeboard. It's filled with a mosaic of empty seed packets and labels. I reach over so I can pin the photograph of the forgiveness machine up over the top of the seed packets, and that's when I notice the small photograph camouflaged in the middle of them. It's William, as an old man, leaning on his stick. He's standing outside in the walled garden. There are summer vegetables behind him in rows. And beside him, grinning, is the man-boy, Anthony, Mary's adult son. The two of them are dressed in baggy gardening trousers and heavy boots. I turn round and look back past the door. William's line of boots sits in the rack where they always are. I move over to them. I lift the first pair out from the rack and turn them over. They are damp. The cold earth trapped between the patterned segs of the soles is still moist. It hasn't hardened yet into a crust.

Down in the field, I find the gate left open. I remember now that I forgot to fasten it shut the last time I was down here. The man-boy must have walked through. He must still have a key for the outhouse. I realize that the footprints in the soil are William's boots, but they are the man-boy's footsteps. I push the gate shut and check that the bar is fastened securely on the latch.

Sorry, we don't have a William Crosby at Hope House.

Senior Care Assistant,
Jane Corrigan

Dear Mary,

I am concerned that your son, Anthony, has been trespassing on our land. It's not that he's done any damage or anything like that. But it was worrying for my daughter to find his footsteps in the soil and to see that he'd been in the outhouse. You will appreciate our wish for privacy after what has been a difficult time for us. I realize that we were a little bit to blame for accidentally leaving the gate open at the bottom of the field. But it is still our land and he really shouldn't be trespassing on it. To make sure it doesn't happen again I have bought a padlock to secure the gate. If you could speak to your son to remind him to stay off our land we would be very grateful.
Yours faithfully,

M. de Bruin

Dear sir,

William Crosby is not a client of ours.

Anne Maguire.
Beechwood Nursing Home

How each atom can be almost all empty space even in solid things
Leaving the bottom gate open in the field
Speaking out loud to Sadie

Each day, in reply to my enquiries, responses come back saying William Crosby isn't a resident of that particular care home. Each day I plant new lines of seeds, new tubers, new sets, following William's plan as though it was 1972 again and William himself had emerged through a wormhole and was pushing each seed into the earth. Each day I extend the scaffolding of twigs and poles linked with lines of string that will hold his plants as they grow; each day the crow's nest up in the tree grows sturdier.

How do you know if you're properly happy? I texted 266.

I don't know that you do, was the reply I got a day later. *I think perhaps you only recognize it afterwards when you're looking back on things.*

29

My dear girl,

Did I tell you that I fell in love with her in Italy? I could tell you what time it was when it happened. I could stand by the very tree I was leaning against.

Our mission down into Italy was opportune. One of the Allied commanders had made a tour of the camp and unnerved the Cossacks by describing them in passing conversation as 'prisoners'. Rumours still persisted in the camp of groups of Georgians and Caucasians elsewhere in the region being handed over against their will to Stalin's Red Army, and General Domanov was still waiting patiently for Field Marshal Alexander to confirm the Cossacks' right to settle in the West. There was a mood of restiveness in the camp, which concerned us all, not least because, for the time being, the Cossacks had been allowed to keep their arms, and any kind of insurrection was the last thing the Allies wanted. Then, helpfully, rumours began to circulate that the Allies were considering forming the Cossack army into a British equivalent of the French Foreign Legion. And, after that, came news of a 'vacant' tract of land on Italy's north-eastern border with Yugoslavia. It was, I was told, about the size of San Marino, another enclave surrounded wholly by Italian land. It was in an area considered 'fluid' by the Allies in terms of resettlement and the drawing of post-war boundaries, and it was in danger of being overrun by Tito's ambitions to swell the size of a communist Yugoslavia.

I was ordered to take my interpreter and two Cossack

representatives selected by General Domanov – Colonel Vasilenko and Dmitri Sukalo, one of Domanov's staff, the dour young man with the sour face and the heavy scar running in a clean line from his temple to the cleft of his chin. Our task was to visit the site in northern Italy and report back on its suitability as a possible location for the Cossack enclave.

It took most of the day to drive there, in a convoy of three vehicles, back through the Plöckenpass. I drove one of the jeeps, with Anna and the boy in the back. The colonel travelled behind in the Fiat being driven by the silent Sukalo, and a couple of corporals from my division rode at the rear as insurance against any difficulties with looters, or with the more organized groups of bandits operating in the mountain passes. We drove down through Tolmezzo and onto the plain, turning east before Udine. By now we were regularly passing lines of civilians walking on the dusty roads in either direction, and men in ones and twos scavenging for wood or chickens, or for whatever could be carried away from undefended yards or empty properties.

The Villa San Lorenzo lay at the head of a long valley. The villa itself and much of the surrounding valley had been owned by Francesco Tuzzo, a Milanese financier who had been one of Mussolini's leading backers. The villa was unoccupied and had been damaged as a result of several raids, probably carried out by Tito's partisans, since the border with Yugoslavia was only a few miles away.

We arrived as the sun was going down. We walked through the ruined house to the rear and stood as a small group on the flagged patio. We looked out at a garden of lemon trees and, beyond it, lines of cypresses forming a long avenue with green folds of land running on to the distant horizon. One of the corporals made some crude remark about Mussolini's friends. His partner guffawed, but the Cossacks stood in silence by the balustrade looking out at the scene. I thought about how far they had come, how long they had fought. A phrase came to me from the bible – of a people coming upon a land flowing with milk and honey.

'Would you be happy to settle here, Colonel?' I asked, pleased with myself that I could offer such a gift to Vasilenko and his comrades.

Anna translated the question for me.

'We must look at the land tomorrow,' was all Vasilenko would commit himself to.

'I wonder if a part of you might prefer to be returning to Russia.'

Anna translated again. Unexpectedly, it was Sukalo who answered me. I realized it was the first time I had heard him speak.

'What did he say?' I asked.

'He said he would rather face death than go to Russia.'

'But Russia is still your home. You wouldn't ever want to go home?'

'I cannot ask him that,' Anna said.

'Why not?'

'Because there is no home. There is no Russia any more. Stalin's thugs have ransacked it. The best that any Cossack could hope for if he was made to go back to Russia is a labour camp.'

'Because some Cossacks fought with the Germans?'

'Because we are Cossacks. Now I think we should talk of something else before the colonel becomes upset.'

'Will you ask Sukalo one more question for me?' I said.

'What?'

'Will you ask him how he got his scar?'

She asked, and Sukalo replied. After the final word he spat onto the ground.

'He says Stalin gave it to him,' Anna said.

'In a battle?'

'In one of his interrogation rooms.'

Before darkness fell I made a check for mines and booby traps around the villa with the two corporals. There was no water or electricity. We agreed to begin a full survey of the estate after breakfast and to make the return journey the day after that, so that a report could be made to General Domanov. I organized the colonel and the other men into those first-floor bedrooms which were in reasonable repair. Anna took the boy with her and they slept in the servants' quarters in the attic. I hadn't much sleep in me and read as best I could using the moon's cold light until, eventually, I fell asleep on the couch.

When I awoke, it was still early. Sunlight was streaming in through the long windows. I walked outside. The land around me smelled of summer and of citrus. I heard the rhythm of a water pump. I walked across the patio and down the stone steps leading to the lemon grove. I walked round to the side of the house and stood by an ancient fig tree looking across into the stable yard. I saw that Anna had found a pump dispensing water from a tap in the middle of the yard. I realized that water would once have been drawn here for horses that now were long gone. Anna was sluicing herself with handfuls of water from a wooden bucket. She was naked. She rubbed at her face, her hair. I didn't know whether I wanted her to see me. I watched the curve of her, the narrowness and flow of her. She stood drying herself with a blanket. I imagined myself standing behind her. I thought of my hands on her. I thought of easing her legs apart, of slipping into her. She glanced round on an instinct and caught sight of me. Behind me, I heard the faintness of a step some distance away. I looked down the valley towards the noise I had heard and saw the boy, playing, down among the villa's avenue of cypresses. He looked up at me and waved.

30

EXILED PERMANENTLY TO HIS Pennine hill, the only place William misses is the little Italian restaurant down in the town. Once or twice a week in the decade since Margaret died he had gone there, ordered a bowl of pasta and a glass of Valpolicella, stayed for an hour, no more. He read from whichever book he had taken that evening. He left quietly and walked back up the hill. They knew to keep the small table at the back of the room for him. If they caught his eye as they moved in and out of the kitchen they would offer him small asides about family or business, treat him as one of them. In return, he tipped well. He knew he had bought their comradeship. It mattered less after Gennaro, the patron, invited him to join the weekly poker game at Maurice's house. The week before Gennaro's offer, returning to his seat from the washroom, he had been standing in front of the obligatory map of Italy that most Italian restaurants seemed to have somewhere on the wall.

'Our family is from Bari,' Gennaro had told him, pointing on the booted outline of the Italian map to the ankle, as if every night he returned home to a house not on the outskirts of Manchester but on an Adriatic hillside in Puglia.

'There was a funny little lighthouse on the harbour at Bari.'

'Are you sure – at Bari?'

'In 1943,' William had said, 'before the ammunition ship exploded in the harbour.' And then he made his way back to his table.

◆ ◆ ◆

He fancies that his organs are thinning down to pulp, his joints calcifying. If he was squeezed, he thinks, he would produce two neat piles – one of sludge and one of powdered stone. Sometimes at night in bed he feels something like meteor showers in his darkened head. If they get too bad he cries out for Irena to come. He hears the soft padding of her feet down the stairs and she sits with him until it passes. No matter how softly he shouts, he realizes, she always hears him.

One afternoon, his son turns up at the farm. William hears the swish of the Audi's impatient tyres in the drive. It makes him smile to think his hearing is unaffected. He is sitting out in the walled garden. Anthony is weeding for him between the rows of vegetables and ripening fruit bushes. William tells him when it's time to stop for an apple juice (he gets Irena to buy them in for him in bulk), otherwise the boy would work on without a break until dusk. Anthony stands drinking the juice, panting happily like a gundog, waiting to be unleashed again.

Kevin's car door shuts with a soft, expensive thud. William hears footsteps approaching.

'Knew we'd be round here, did you?'

Kevin sees the wheelchair. 'Jesus, Dad, what happened? Why didn't you tell us?'

William looks down at the chair as if it takes him by surprise, too. He raises his head. 'We use it for chariot racing, Anthony, don't we?'

Anthony looks up at him briefly and grins.

'To what do we owe the honour?' William says.

'Will you tell me what happened?' Kevin asks, still looking at the chair.

'I got old. That's what happened.'

'Did you have a fall or something?'

'More fun than that. I had a stroke.'

'You had a stroke? Why didn't they tell me? No one told me.'

'I didn't want to tell you. Why should I tell you? You going to come and tuck me in bed at night? Your po-faced wife going to bake me cakes?'

'It's not blunted your tongue, then, this stroke.'

'No, that was a silver lining.'

'When did it happen?'

'A few weeks ago.'

'Well, shouldn't you be in a… how can you live up here on your own? Don't they have people…'

'I don't want to move. And I'm not on my own. I have Anthony to help me.'

'Jesus, Dad, don't be stupid, he's a…'

'… good worker is Anthony. Aren't you, Anthony? A good worker.'

Anthony nods briefly, distracted from his task.

'But what about your care? You can't live alone. You said yourself, you're getting old. We should be making some arrangement.'

'I don't live alone.'

'You don't?'

'I live with Irena, now.'

'Who's Irena?'

'She's watching you from the kitchen window. She's trying to work out whether you're friend or foe.'

Kevin turns and sees Irena at the sink. Her face makes no inflection.

'Who is Irena?'

'She's a gypsy,' William says. 'She's come to steal all my money when I'm too infirm, so there'll be none for you.'

'Don't be crass. Who is she?'

'I told you, she lives here.'

'Has she been vetted?'

'How should I know? I'm the police now?'

'I want you to give me the name of the company she works for, Dad. I want to check her out.'

'And I want to get up out of this chair and dance the fucking bossa nova round the rhubarb.'

And so it goes on for five minutes more. William throwing darts of spite; Kevin, in his accountant's pale grey suit, alternately playing patronizing adult and piqued child, until, glancing at the balance sheet, he recognizes there is nothing here for him and reconciles himself to telling Penny that he's had a go and got precisely nowhere.

William watches the Audi drive, too quickly, down the track, throwing up spirals of late summer dust in its wake. It makes him think of Brody's one and only visit here, when Becky was a toddler and Kevin, pale faced and earnest at twelve or thirteen, had burst into tears when William had raised his voice to a visitor he didn't know.

Brody had turned up on a day like this. It was a Sunday. He had walked up from the town, dishevelled, sweating in the heat with a jacket over his shoulder and sporting several days of stubble. He had that odour on him that came from spending hours sitting motionless in public carriages. William recognized it from the war. Somehow Brody had made the wrong turn coming up from the town, following somebody's directions, and William and the children spotted him striding long-legged up the field.

'This is my friend, Joseph Brody,' William had said cautiously after they had shaken hands. 'We were together in the war.' He realized how unfamiliar the word 'Joseph' was in his mouth.

'You were in the war?' Kevin asked.

'Not really,' William said. 'Not much.'

'Nice place,' Brody said looking round, seeming oblivious to the children.

'You look…' William began.

'Terrible. I'm sorry. Look, I should have let you know,

told you I was coming. Rung you or something. If I had your number.'

'I should... get you tea or something,' William said.

'Tea, yes. Let's have tea. Then these fine children can tell me all about themselves.'

Brody, it turned out, had released himself from hospital. His wife had left him and taken their children. He had become impossible to live with. She had met someone else.

'How did you get here?' William said.

'Walked,' Brody said, with a little too much energy. 'Walked, hitched, you know. Three days I think. Had enough change for a couple of buses along the way.' He shrugged at the nonsense of it.

'How will you get back? To Scotland? It is still Scotland?'

Brody puzzled at the question. 'Don't know,' he said, as if it was of no consequence.

It turned out he wanted to talk about the war. He'd got this idea in the hospital that he wanted William's forgiveness for something.

'You saved my life and I never told you that.'

William shrugged awkwardly to indicate that this was enough.

But Brody wouldn't stop there. In the kitchen he became more animated. He hadn't discharged himself and walked from Scotland to stop there. He wanted to share things with William that he had bottled up for years. And William, who had declined every petition Brody had ever made to go to reunions, whose Christmas cards to him were more about Margaret's clerical thoroughness over the list, whose messages of festive goodwill were terse and business-like – 'To Joseph, Season's Greetings, William, Margaret and the children' – realized that all along he had been right.

'I don't want to talk about this,' he said.

'It *needs* talking about,' Brody said. 'I've spent too long not talking about it. I want to talk.' His voice was rising.

'And I don't,' William said, and he crashed the palm of his hand down on the kitchen table. Margaret was gripping a tea towel. Kevin, beside her, began to cry. William stood up to feel in his wallet for money to give him and then told Brody that maybe it was time for him to leave.

31

THROUGH THE INTERCOM, Sadie says, 'Just try once more.'

With a mouse's keen instinct for these things, I can feel a hint of exasperation in her voice. Like a good professional, Sadie senses it herself and smooths it away.

'Close your eyes for a moment,' she says, 'and see if you can picture Max sitting there in the room with you. Then open your eyes and read your sentence quietly to him. I'm going to turn off the intercom now, so even I won't be able to hear you. It'll just be you and Max.'

I hear a click. I know this is meant to be the intercom being switched off. I wonder if it's really off. I'm not so sure. I know, after all, that Sadie isn't all she seems. I close my eyes. I try to picture Max with me in the small room adjacent to Sadie's office. I see him watching me. He's grinning. He's assuring me that there's nothing to it. Come on, Mouse, he says, with that same flicker of frustration that I heard in Sadie's voice. I open my eyes and begin to read from the page.

'I mourn for the bees. They have been tormented to death by the warring armies. In Volhynia there are no more bees.'

I finish reading the passage from the Isaac Babel story. Like the other stories in the book, they don't yet make much sense to me, but I am persisting with them. The only sound in the room is the background hum of the air conditioning. My lips moved, my chest heaved and punched at the words, but my throat was tight. I couldn't clench or grip the sounds and each one leaked away, leaving only the air conditioning's drone. When I look across the room in my mind's eye I see that Max has gone and I am alone.

When I go back into Sadie's office she is determinedly upbeat. 'So, how are the plans for looking at schools coming on?' But she is a little forced in her jollity. I have let her down, I know. I can't help it. I am trying. I give a kind of shrug in response to her question, trying to convey a sense that the whole school thing is, of course, getting all the attention it most definitely deserves.

'Will you and your mum be looking for a school you can travel to from the farm, or will you be moving again in the summer?'

I think we'll be staying there, I write on the whiteboard.

'And the schools?' Sadie says, persisting gently.

There are other things to worry about as well as schools, I write.

'But it will need sorting, Mouse, won't it? About school.'

We're thinking that Mum might carry on home educating me, I write.

'We?'

Me and Mum.

I want to write, *Who do you think?* as well, but I stop myself.

'You've talked about this, the two of you?'

I told you, I write, then I wipe the sentence from the whiteboard almost before Sadie can read it.

'And Mum agrees with you? About home educating rather than going back to school in September?'

I write, *I'm a bit worried about Mum.*

'Why are you worried?'

She needs me to be at home.

'But you need to go to school, Mouse. And I think maybe that's what your mum wants, too.'

You don't know that, I write. I underline the *know*. Because it's true; she doesn't know.

'Is it possible, Mouse, that it's hard for her to be as strong with you as she'd like to be?'

I think I know Mum better than you do, I write.

'So, have the education welfare people been in touch lately? Phoned maybe? Or written?'

I shrug and shake my head in a single movement.

'Has your dad been in touch?'

I don't want to talk about that.

'Okay, Mouse, okay. That's fine. So you tell me what you'd like us to talk about. How about Lucas?'

I shake my head.

'Max? What about Max?'

NO! I write.

There is a pause while Sadie regroups.

'Tell me what you're up to at the farm,' she says eventually.

There's not much to tell, I write, grateful at least for the chance to wipe clean the shouted *NO!* I'm starting to feel trapped.

Is it time to go yet? I write.

'Not yet,' Sadie says. She's in no rush. And why not. She's getting paid to sit here failing to teach me how to speak and getting twitchy as if it's my fault and not hers, and pretending that all she's interested in is getting sounds to come out of my mouth. And so I spend the next twenty minutes not telling her about why I chose to read out loud from a short story written by Isaac Babel, or where the book came from. I don't tell her about the fox I've seen three times now on our land, or the single word that came out of my mouth the first time I saw it. I don't say anything about the letter that arrived for William yesterday.

I walk back into Piccadilly Gardens. A watery sun spills its warmth on the city as I sit down by the statue where, two months ago, Lucas sat and I hung back at the edge of the square waiting patiently to avoid him. I haven't heard from Lucas lately. I told him that maybe we could meet up over the summer. We might be settled then, I said. Perhaps the troupe of performers from Circus Malmedy might have resolved their legal wranglings by then and paid off their creditors and be out on the road again. Then Mum and I can finally be free of them I said, as lightly and sincerely as I could. But there was no reply.

I walk into the coffee house. There's no sign of Pavel today. I have my piece of paper from the Filofax ready.

One small hot chocolate and a lemon muffin to take away please.

I don't have long enough to eat in today, even with the extra time I negotiated with Mum for 'window shopping'.

Standing in the queue, I feel the vibration of my phone. I slip it out of my pocket and see that there's a text from 266. We've been texting in the last few days about different things that make us nervous. It started after she told me about the forgiveness machine that Karen Green invented when her partner died. I wondered what her husband, the writer, could have been so frightened of that he stayed at home so much and took medication. 266 said I'd be surprised at how many things people are frightened of, which she guessed I would find out about as I grew up. Which puzzled me, because I'd never said to 266 that I was only eleven and I think I tend to hide my age quite well when I'm texting or emailing. So I admitted that my mum and I were renting a farmhouse and I'd had this idea that, when we had enough money, I would build a fence right round its perimeter and have a watchtower so we could keep people out.

The text says, *I seem to recall there was a famous writer who tried that once.*

'Can I help you?' a voice says, a bit too briskly. I look up. The new barista looks flushed in the face and cross, like he's struggling to keep up. I hand my piece of paper over to him and slide my money down in a pile on the counter. The barista spreads it suspiciously, then takes it with a reluctant sweep of his hand like I might be on some sort of Rag Week stunt or, worse, someone with no English trying to pass off foreign currency. He turns his attention towards the man in the suit waiting behind me in the queue and smiles nicely for him. I decide not to leave him a tip.

When my order is ready, I carry my drink and muffin across to the Metro platform, buy my ticket with the small amount of shopping money Mum gave me (because shopping in the city for an hour is a *good thing*) and wait on the unfamiliar side of the track for the Eccles tram. It arrives a few minutes later. I find a seat and the tram glides away, past the shops of Mosley Street and out towards Trafford. I watch people hustling past each other on the pavement. I pull out the letter that arrived this week at the farm. It says that, 'Regrettably, we must announce a rise in your nursing fees at Beardwood House.' There are some calculations, and an explanation that this is the first rise in the rates charged by the home in over twelve months. The letter is addressed to Mr William Crosby at Bank Hey Farm. The letter has been cc'ed at the bottom to Mr Kevin Crosby.

I check through the details once more, even though I've read the letter seven times since it arrived, five times before I emailed the home yesterday and two times this morning before I set off. It's pretty clear that it's an administrative error. Someone in an office tasked with writing to each of the residents, and with sending copies to each family contact, has clicked on the wrong address and sent William's own copy out in the post to the home address he was registered as living at when he entered Beardwood. Above the letter are the embossed details of the home: its address, phone number, website and email. I sent them an email yesterday afternoon:

> Dear Beardwood Nursing Home,
>
> I am a longstanding friend of William Crosby, who I believe is a resident in your nursing home. We were comrades together in the war. Although I live in Scotland and am too elderly to visit him myself, my granddaughter is in

> Manchester staying with friends and would like to visit William, who she looks upon as her uncle. I am letting you know because she has a condition which means she has no speech and I wanted to let you know about this in advance. If you could let us know if there are visiting times or when my granddaughter could visit we would be very grateful.
>
> Yours sincerely,
> Joseph Brody

I get off the tram and follow the street map I printed off last night. Beardwood Nursing Home is a large modern building set back from the road with a sweeping drive and a car park in front of a porch entrance, which has a key pad and a buzzer. I step off the pavement and hang back on the edge of the drive. I stand looking across at the porch, at the intercom, at the locked door. I slip out of sight of anyone looking out from the home into the shadow of the shrubbery.

Which is scariest, sharks or new places? I type. I scroll down my list of contacts to 266 and press 'send'. I can feel my stomach tighten. The fact that I have actually come here planning to meet with William Crosby has turned being nervous into a real, physical thing. I spent last night writing down fourteen questions for him in my Filofax, but what will I do if he doesn't want to answer them? If he's not interested in the new season's planting in the walled garden or the box of photographs and mementoes sent to me by Joseph Brody's daughter, some of which I've brought in my rucksack. Maybe he'll be different to the person I've been imagining all this time, the one who's still a boy in shorts, my age inside his old man's body. This is a man, after all, who thinks his son is an idiot, who nailed a sheep's heart to a door, who wouldn't go to Joseph Brody's funeral or write to Brody's daughter after he died. Maybe this William Crosby will shout angrily for help; maybe the staff will call the police; maybe Joseph Brody's daughter will be forced to confirm that I'm a fake. And that's when I realize that in fact I don't want to go any further. What I most want is to head back to the Metro stop and catch the next tram back into the city. I want to meet up with Mum and go home, forget about William Crosby, at least the one who's here in a room at Beardwood House. I realize with relief that there's nothing to stop me walking away. I start to feel a whole lot better. I feel absolved. I step out from the shrubbery, and a Range Rover whipping smoothly round the tight bend from the road into the drive has to slam to a juddering halt to avoid hitting me, tyres smoking on the gravel, accusing headlights screaming light into my face. It's close enough for my outstretched hand to be touching the warm metal of the bonnet. I can't move. I stand frozen to the spot, wrenched from the vagueness of my daydreaming. My eyes are fixed on the bonnet of the car. When I glance up, I see that the man behind the wheel is saying the F word at me. He jams the car into reverse. The skid of the wheels as it reverses makes me jump. The driver steers round me, faster than he needs to, still mouthing swear words that are lost behind the windscreen glass and the rhythmic thud of the car's music system that I can feel as a pulse inside my chest. I edge back into the shadow of the shrubbery. I feel myself starting to shake. I sit down on the ground.

I'm still shaking a moment later when one of the uniformed staff emerges from the front door of the nursing home and walks over to me. She crouches down so she is almost level with me. I wonder if she is going to tell me off for walking in front of the Range Rover, or ask me to leave the grounds because they're private property.

'I hear you've been stopping the traffic,' she says, smiling.

I look at her.

She produces a sheet of paper and holds it out for me. On it is written, 'Are you Mr Brody's granddaughter?' I'm so relieved that it takes me a moment before I can think to pull out my Filofax and write down: *My ears are fine. It's just my voice that doesn't work.*

◆ ◆ ◆

I stand at the edge of the room alongside the woman in the uniform, who tells me to call her Alice. This is William's room, the one he has now at Beardwood Nursing Home. A metal stand holds a bag of clear fluid with a tube running from it down to the sleeping figure in the bed. His curled shape occupies less space under the quilt than I thought it would. I think of the shape of William's big boots pressed into the earth next to the early broad bean shoots in the walled garden. I think of the man in the photograph that Joseph Brody's daughter sent me of him and William as young men squatting side by side on the bonnet of a jeep in wartime Italy.

'He's being peg fed,' Alice says.

I look at her.

'The peg takes the food into his tummy. It doesn't hurt him. It just gives him a steady supply of nourishment because he's not able to eat on his own.'

I write a note. *Is he asleep?*

She nods. 'He's like this mostly now. It's like a coma. You've heard of people being in comas?'

Does he hear things?

'That's hard to say, really. We get little reactions sometimes, but he's not conscious very much, so it's only guesswork as to how much is going in. We're not even sure if people dream when they're like this. And there aren't many visitors. William's son only comes once in a while, and he's not a great one for chit-chat. I like to talk to them anyway, even if everything isn't going in. I think the sound of a voice can sometimes help. And I think the person your uncle was is still in there somewhere. I like to think that he's just dreaming. Is it a bit scary seeing him like this?'

I shake my head. It's not scary. It doesn't feel at all scary now she has explained about the peg feed. It's just too late, is what it is.

32

MARY'S 'CHANCE ENCOUNTER' STORY featured a girl who lived somewhere more or less where Mary did, who was more or less Mary's age when it happened, who seemed to think and sound like her, as far as the other members of the writing group could judge.

The girl in the story was being tutored for the Oxbridge examination. She walked up the hill twice a week after her sixth-form classes were over for the day to meet an English teacher who lived in a big house above the town and who taught at a grammar school in the city. After each lesson, she found she was looking forward to the next one, not because the English teacher was kind, or complimented her, or made her feel especially bright, but because she could feel a new way of looking at the world opening up inside her.

She studied the books of essays, remembering the causes the writers championed. She read and tried to memorize the plots of novels he set her to read. But the man didn't ask about these things. Instead, he was curious to know what opinion she had formed about the writer, why they thought like that, or wrote like that, whether she would have acted in the same way as a character had, whether an author liked his characters.

There was little small talk when the girl in the story arrived for her tutorials. She wasn't asked if she was well or what she had been up to. When it rained the man would offer to drive her back down into the town after the lesson, and that was the only time he would talk about himself, or would ask the girl one or two questions about her own life away from her studies.

In the story, the girl didn't know much about the man. She had learned that he wrote poetry; that twenty years ago, during the war, when he had been in the army, he had entertained thoughts of making his living as a writer; that teaching was an acceptable sort of job; that most of the boys at the school were pleasant and most of the masters were stupid and that he disliked the head, whom he thought arrogant and complacent and dull. She knew he was married and had children. Sometimes he heard the children playing elsewhere in the house. This was all the girl knew about him, but despite this it didn't shock her when he kissed her. She was standing at a bus stop in Manchester one drizzly evening when he pulled over and offered her a lift home. At the end of her road, where he had stopped the car, they talked for a while and then he leaned across and kissed her on the lips.

The girl in the story knew she was pretty. She knew that boys at school were attracted to her. She had been out with a few, but not gone all the way. But it wasn't only her prettiness that caused her not to be surprised when he kissed her. It had seemed, somehow, inevitable. She realized she had been waiting for it and she welcomed the kiss and pushed back into him in the car.

'You know I'm married?' he said.

The girl in the story nodded. She was breathing faster now. She recognized that she wanted him more than she wanted any of the boys in the town who flattered her and, on dates, pawed sheepishly at her. He slipped a hand beneath her coat and found the button of her shirt. She felt the sensation of his fingertips slide across her stomach with an explosion of ecstasy and panic because she wasn't sure what came next. She leaned across and found his mouth again with hers and he drove them to a quiet parking place in the hills, and so it was for several weeks, secretly, dangerously, pleasurably, until, a few days after her Oxbridge examination, he called a halt to things, not meaning to hurt her, he said, not wanting to be unkind, not wanting her to believe that it could lead to anything more.

It was this that led the girl in the story to want one of the boys in the town. He had pursued her so diligently, flattered her, rejected other girls in forlorn pursuit of her that she let him corner her one day in the school grounds and drew a delicate finger slowly down the length of his crotch and watched him judder and melt in front of her. The power that she had entranced her and soothed the pain she felt every time she glanced upwards after that at the farmhouse on the hill.

Mary finished reading her story. Someone coughed. Before the tutor intervened to thank her, there was a short, intense silence, which spoke of how much the others had been made uncomfortable by what she had written. It wasn't, they were clear, what they came to the group for.

33

My dear girl,

There are times when I tell myself I must have dreamed the Villa San Lorenzo, how I came to be there in the aftermath of war with a woman who led me to the stable block after supper on our second night, who took my face in her hands and kissed me.

'You see how simple things can be,' she said, as if what she had done was hardly anything at all.

'I do,' I told her. I did see. I believed her.

She had settled the boy, Leo, upstairs in their attic room. I had allowed the two corporals to take a jeep to drive into the nearest local village for the evening to see what distractions they could find to amuse themselves. Vasilenko and Sukalo were drinking vodka and playing cards in the ransacked drawing room with its upended piano and obscene graffiti carved into the mahogany table with a knife. We had one further day's work ahead of us to complete our survey of the estates to assess whether it might provide the pastureland and the acres to cultivate that the Cossacks needed.

Anna had found a wind-up gramophone and a collection of records, overlooked or disregarded in the raids by Tito's Partisans. Improbably, as we slipped them from their dust sleeves, we saw that most of them were American songs – Irving Berlin, Hoagy Carmichael, the Gershwins. We carried them out onto the patio and danced a little to 'Cheek to Cheek' and 'How Long Has This Been Going On?' I pressed my head into her neck and drank the scent of her; I who had given up believing in the mud below the monastery at Monte Cassino that I would last another day.

'We'll grow old here together,' I told her.

'You shouldn't make promises,' she said.

'I should,' I told her. 'I must.'

It seemed to me that making promises was part of the covenant I was making to return to the civilized world. Promises showed that it was possible to look ahead to something beyond the next fox hole, the next meal, the next casual death. Promises felt like the necessary signal of the return of hope.

I told her about the geography of Italy. I described the spine of mountains running down its length. I told her this in whispers. The geography of Italy, I said, is like a fishbone. Trying to conquer it from south to north involves cresting one bony horizontal ridge after another in order to reach the town at the summit, then descending into the valley on the other side, crossing the river and climbing again. Each hilltop town, I told her, is a medieval fortress, its defences refined over a thousand years of sieges, the kind first waged with bows and arrows, and latterly with mortars and air support, with the flooding of rivers, the blowing of dams, the mining of bridges, and roads, and the corpses of dead Italians hung from trees or lampposts. On the slopes of mountains, in the chaos of war, in driving sleet, in mist, in the cut and thrust of assault and counterattack, men can easily become separated from their divisions, I said, can become lost beyond their lines in fox holes, sometimes for days. In winter, I said, this warfare in Italy means trenches half-filled with water. Rain and snow. Your hands go blue with the cold. You wake from sleep, I told her, and your breath has formed into beads of ice on the blanket. Your feet swell, I said, and then trench foot sets in. Men stop reacting to their surroundings in those circumstances. Brody and I had a single wet blanket each. For two nights in the slit trench we slept huddled together to keep warm. In the end, I told her, Brody simply wanted to go to sleep. He'd had enough. The human body, I said, is designed for fight or flight, but sometimes a third strategy kicks in and it freezes, like a car stuck between gears. Brody was too chilled, too numb, to think for himself. In the end, he felt his God had deserted him. I was smaller than him, slighter, less bodyweight. Less troubled by belief in an absenting God. At the end of the second night, under cover of the mortar shells that were splintering the trees a hundred yards away, I dragged him down the hill towards our lines.

I told her that, at this point, we hadn't even heard of Cassino. That was still to come. We thought we were close to the end when in fact we had barely started. You must remember, I told her, that Monte Cassino, which later on historians would argue had rivalled Stalingrad in its scale, would swallow us for six months as the Germans tried to bar our way north to Rome. Men stopped expecting to survive. It was no longer possible to look forwards into the future, only to look back.

Afterwards, we fell asleep. We were in the hayloft above the stables. She had thought to bring blankets. She knew it would happen. She felt so light against me, a negligible weight, naked against my skin. I woke suddenly, afraid of where I was, waiting anxiously for the crack of mortars, and there she was breathing deeply, her sleep a rebuke to me, and I realized I could look ahead of me, a day, two days, a week. Eventually, a lifetime would stretch ahead of us. I lay as still as I could. I didn't want to wake her. I wanted to stay like this for ever.

34

THE SUN COMES UP a little earlier each day and sinks behind the hills a little later. The soil becomes a little warmer to the touch; gooseberries swell on bushes; vegetable grow in William's ground; patterns of broad beans and summer cabbage and peas following the lines he sketched out for the summer of 1972 when he and the eleven-year-old Rebecca tended to everything that had weathered the late frosts, evaded the garden's army of slugs, survived the pheasants and the pigeons gorging on young shoots. Now, in place of William and Rebecca, it has become my job to watch over them.

I work alone. I've been undisturbed in the walled garden ever since I fastened the gate at the bottom of the field with a length of blue nylon rope, and changed the padlock on the outhouse. I wrote complaining to the man-boy's mother about him. There have been no more footprints in the earth; no more wet boots left drying on the shoe rack in the outhouse. His mother didn't respond to my latest letter. I think I made my point, so that's an end to it. I still catch sight of him standing sentry at his post at the bottom of the field, arms looped over the barred gate, but I try to make it look like I haven't spotted him. I turn away and reassure myself that this isn't his land.

Mum tells me one evening over supper that she is going back to work. She speaks the words like she's been practising them. She says it like I might be a bit interested in this news, but not much. I try not to show how concerned I am. I haven't seen this coming. Nothing has changed as far as I can see. She still lives on soup, and painted trees, and forgets to set me home education work, or forgets to mark it. And I know that the owls still keep her awake at night.

It might be too soon, I write.

'I think it's been long enough,' she says.

You could work from home, I write.

'I think it might be good for me to be with people,' she says. 'Just a little.'

I'm people, I write.

'Oh, my poor Mouse,' she says, and gives me a hug. I think she means that I'm not *enough* people. I want to ask if Max would have been *enough*.

Two hours? I query.

'That's all,' she says. 'Just to get used to it for a while. So we don't have to keep asking your dad for money. So we have enough money ourselves to pay the rent.'

I go away to my room to think about it. I pull on William's cardigan. I stand in his shoes. I can't see why my dad shouldn't keep paying us money. It's the least he can do. But I avoid saying this to Mum. Thinking hard about it, I decide that it could be a good thing. We could save the money my dad pays to Mum. She could go out to work maybe once a week so she could see *enough* people and still home educate me. Maybe Mum's salary and the money from my dad would mean we wouldn't need to live off our savings any more. We could buy the farm when our house on the avenue is sold. I think about how we could grow all the vegetables we'd need. We could keep chickens. We could pay to have workmen build a watch-tower to keep trespassers out. I could practise writing stories undisturbed, Mum would paint, and we'd use the watchtower to maintain our privacy, and people would stop sending us letters and finally learn to leave us alone.

On each Tuesday afternoon, when Mum goes to her office, I

sit with the sleeping William for an hour in the nursing home. After lunch we drive down from the farm, park at the Metro terminus and ride into the city together. Mum gets off at Piccadilly Gardens and walks down towards the glass-fronted offices of the chambers near the railway station where she has worked for sixteen years, except for the year that Max was born and the year that I was born, and where, in place of painting lines of winter trees on stretched white canvases, she has resumed working for a couple of hours each week as a barrister. I stay on the tram until my own stop in the suburbs and then make the three turns on foot until, unknown to Mum who thinks I've gone into the city to window shop, I reach the driveway of Beardwood House.

I wanted to let William know about the fox that showed up at the farm. I wanted to ask if he had ever seen it. I wanted to tell him about the pair of crows who have built their nest in the copse this spring. I wanted to show him the photographs that Joseph Brody's daughter sent in the post. I planned to let him see the diary Joseph kept in the war that's hard to read because it's in such small handwriting. Instead, because William can't see them, I've pinned them up in my bedroom. The wall is more than half full now. There are still gaps – spaces to fill, things I don't know. I wanted to ask William what happened in the war; why he wouldn't ever go to army reunions; why he didn't go to the funeral of his friend, Joseph Brody.

I asked Alice what I should do in the room while the tube drips food into William's stomach, keeping him alive. I made a note that Alice is a 7.2. She likes her job. None of the old people upset her, even when one of them gets confused and shouts out, or stumbles in a corridor. Bring a book to keep yourself amused, she said. It's enough that you're there in the room with him. It's enough that somebody's there.

Since William can't speak any more, I thought it would be nice to bring with me some of the things he wrote, and so, while he sleeps on, I read them to myself, because Alice told me that this is enough.

When I enter William's room this afternoon, one of his feet has slipped out from the quilt. I look at it for a while. There is no padding of spare flesh. It's just ligament and bone; white skin, blue veins. I lift the sheet to reposition it over him. In lifting it, I see the narrow curl of his body; I catch his warm animal scent. One pyjama leg has ridden up to the knee. I see skin like crêpe paper stretched over the shin bone. If you held it up to the light, you could surely see through it, as if he's already started to be not physically here. I don't know what score he would be. I'm not sure you can calculate a score for someone who just sleeps, who feels no pain but nothing good, either. It would help to know what he is dreaming about. Alice says a coma is sometimes a way for the human body, when it's very old like this, to prepare to die. I think she's preparing me, too, to make sure I don't get upset when William dies. When she talks about him she still says 'your uncle'. I don't think I'll tell her the truth. I don't think it would help.

A text comes in on my phone from 266.

I remembered about the watchtower, the text says. *It was J. D. Salinger. He built it on his land in the New Hampshire woods.*

I send a reply to 266. *Why did J. D. Salinger want to keep people out?*

I'm texting more to 266 at the moment, because Lucas has stopped replying to me. I'd grown used to getting at least a couple of texts each day from him. I wrote him a letter telling him that we woke up one morning in our boarding house to find that all the circus people had gone. But Lucas didn't text me back.

The reply from 266 comes in. *He wanted to be left alone. All through the last year of the war he was on the front line. All he wanted afterwards was to write. Sometimes I know how he feels.*

I pull out the Filofax from my coat pocket and make a

note that I should read something by J. D. Salinger. I slide the Filofax back and look around the room. I realize there isn't anything in there that is William's. No photographs. No books. Just clean, wiped surfaces. The things that are his, that he gathered around him during his life, now surround me at the farm. I sit in the chair in the room reading to myself. Now and then I glance up while William sleeps in the bed beside me, immersed in dreams I can't guess at or imagine.

35

My dear girl,

She said to me, 'Why now? It seems such an odd time.'

She was curled against me in my narrow bed in the eaves of our hotel quarters. The boy was asleep under his blankets in the Fiat parked round the back. She was only curious. She had seemed distracted during the day. Not unhappy, but as though a part of her was being unaccountably withheld.

I reassured her. I said the plan was to exchange them all for British arms. What good was a motley collection of sabres and stolen German and Italian handguns and rifles, especially since the British couldn't supply ammunition for all those different kinds of guns? Better all round, I suggested, to give everyone British standard issue.

She nodded vaguely. 'When?' she said. I felt her breath falling softly on my skin.

Before the resettlement, I told her. The British liked to do things properly, I said. Why would they go to the trouble of sending a party to investigate Tuzzo's Italian estate unless the British were serious in their intent to set aside a small piece of land for the Cossacks?

We had reported to the brigade's Lienz HQ about the suitability of Francesco Tuzzo's vast estates running north-east of Udine to the Yugoslav border. General Domanov had seemed satisfied. In the days that followed, our report had helped to quiet the rumblings of discontent around the camp. Patience had been restored. Even the request for the Cossacks to hand in their assorted weaponry had been accepted with equanimity. Now we were waiting for news from Field Marshal Alexander.

By now, Brody knew about Anna and I. If he heard the sound of the Fiat's engine manoeuvring off the road and round to the back of the hotel he would take it upon himself to disappear down into the town for an hour or two. Amid the debris of bully beef and *Daily Mirrors* and Brody's opened, leather-bound bible, in the narrow cradle of a chambermaid's single bed, I took possession of Anna's body. I learned about the colour of her face in darkness, the shapes her small, lithe body made, the sounds escaping from her in muffled cries, the seriousness of her face in sleep, the reshaped lip, the fall of her hair, the slope of shoulders and hips at rest, the promise of the future.

'I am with child,' she said. She didn't say pregnant, she said 'with child'. For a moment I thought she was referring to the boy outside in the car, to Leo, who ran around all day conveying messages for Vasilenko and who slept like a bear at night.

'How can you know?' I asked. 'It's only been…'

'A week,' she said, and she smiled.

'You can't be sure?'

She made a face as if to say what would I know of these things. 'I just know,' she said. 'In the same way that I know it's going to be a girl.'

'I don't know what to say,' I said, 'I…'

'You don't say anything,' she told me. 'This is our secret for now. Our quiet secret, me and you.'

'When?' I said.

'On the first night, in Italy, at Tuzzo's villa.'

'In the barn? The hayloft?' I laughed out loud in joy.

'Sshh,' she scolded, still anxious for the others billeted in the hotel not to know about us yet, and we lapsed again into something close to sleep.

We had spent the day overseeing the handing in of weapons by the Cossacks. Mounds of German, French and Italian arms and ammunition, even Romanian guns taken after the Battle of Stalingrad, grew at designated spots round the valley. Rifles, revolvers, sabres, whatever the Cossacks had been given, or had taken, along the way were thrown onto ever-increasing piles, to be loaded onto British three-tonners and driven away. Beforehand, the British had been nervous about what might happen following the order, but in the event the Cossacks had complied meekly, trustingly.

'You see,' Anna had told me. 'Cossacks are disciplined people.'

I was woken from my half-sleep by the crash of footsteps coming up the wooden stairs. I turned and saw Brody's shape in the doorway.

'Sorry,' he said. He eyed Anna nervously, then turned to me. 'The major wants you. There's a meeting organized tomorrow for the Cossack officers. A sort of conference – with Field Marshal Alexander. He wants you to tell the Cossacks tonight. You'll need Anna with you. Sorry, again.'

I twisted from the bed and sat up.

'That's good,' I said, turning to Anna, who still lay beneath the blanket. 'You see! Alexander's coming here to meet the Cossacks.'

'Not here,' Brody said. 'It's in Oberdrauburg. 'That's where the meeting's going to be. With all the Cossack officers.'

'All of them?'

'Yes, come on, quick sharp. I told the major I'd find you so you can let them know.' Brody left the room. I heard the rat-tat-tat of his boots hurrying down the stairs and I started to get dressed.

'It must be in response to the letters the general sent him,' I said.

'But why Oberdrauburg?' she said. 'Why make two thousand officers travel to Oberdrauburg to meet one field marshal?' She wasn't sleepy any more.

36

IN THE KITCHEN, IRENA reads to him. Now that the sitting room holds his bed, he prefers to stay out of there during the day. The small front room is too cold without the bother of lighting the wood-burning stove, and so they spend their days and evenings in the kitchen. He likes to sit at the table. Anything to be out of the wheelchair. She helps him onto one of the solid chairs which he bought, along with the table, at an auction in Salford in Coronation year. It took four men to manoeuvre the table in through the gap where the window had been.

She is happy to read to him. It helps with her English. He can see enough to read, but the effort of holding a book with his working arm means he can only manage a few minutes at a time before his body needs a rest. While she is out of the house on her other calls for the agency, or shopping – 'You cannot eat this frozen shit, you need vegetables, fresh' – he selects the books for her to read from that evening.

'Sal – in – jair,' he says, correcting her pronunciation.

'J. D. Sal – in – jair,' she tries. '"A Perfect Day for Bananafish." *Bananafish?* What is this?'

He makes a movement of his hand to show it's of no consequence. 'It's not a real fish,' he says. 'Made up.'

She nods that she has understood. She reads the story. He knows pretty much every word. He has read it himself perhaps a hundred times. Only once did he read it to Rebecca, to whom he loved to read. It was a mistake, he realizes, to have read that particular story to her. He should have left her to stumble upon it later in life, when the world had taken divots out of her. She was so horrified by the shooting, by the nonchalance of death.

He wheels himself into his study and returns holding the letter to his daughter that he has been working on for almost a year. He can no longer strike the keys or hold a pen with enough control to write. He asks Irena to make changes, then gets her to read it back to him. He sits, white faced, tense, listening to it read out loud, like a man being charged with drink-driving offences after a crash he can barely remember.

'Throw it away,' he says finally.

'Good,' she says. 'You shouldn't write to her.'

'Why not?'

'You have her phone number?'

'Her mobile. I got one of her friends to give it me, but she won't ever answer if she knows it's me.'

'So ring again, don't write.'

'It's none of your business,' he says coolly.

'I'm just saying,' she says. She finds the number written in the address book he keeps on the stand in the hall.

'What are you doing with that?' he demands as she carries it back into the kitchen.

'I show you,' Irena says. She climbs up onto the kitchen unit and copies out the number in chalk high up on the wall out of his reach, each digit large enough to read from where he sits at the table, finishing the final '6' with a flourish.

'I don't want it there,' he snaps.

She is nonplussed. 'Each time you see it there, it reminds you to ring her, yes?'

'No, rub the damned thing off.'

'I won't.'

She climbs back down to the floor.

'You are my guest in this house. You do as I say. Rub it *off*!'

'Don't think you can treat me like a child. Like some child in your class at school.'

As best he can he aims the cup he has been drinking from, with its dreg of tea, towards her. He hurls it. The cup smacks against the range and breaks on the flagged floor. She steps towards him to calm him, patient at his show of temper. He swings an arm at her, almost a punch, and the back of his hand strikes a glancing blow in her face. Instinctively she gasps and turns away from him. She feels at her face. The wetness is a trace of blood from her nose. The suddenness of the blow surprises them both. He withdraws his arm and cradles it to him, still angry but subdued. She has been hit often enough to recognize the crossing of a boundary, the end of something. The doorbell rings. The noise is startling. They stiffen. Neither of them moves. It's dark outside. Even in daylight there are so few callers. All of them are anticipated. No one wanders up the lane by chance. They have no passers-by or salesmen.

Slowly William edges the wheelchair round and forces it, one-handed, out into the hall towards the door. She lets him do it. She stays in the kitchen. Her heart is beating fast. Blood is dripping from her nose. She wipes it again with the back of her hand, moves over into the doorway, keeping out of sight. She hears William reach up and open the front door. She holds her breath.

She hears William speak first. 'Yes? What is it?'

The shadow at the door speaks. What he says doesn't register with her at first – only the tone, the musicality of the words, which she recognizes as Marco's. The rising panic in her feels like a lack of oxygen. She feels herself sway. She starts to pick out words. Marco asks again if a woman called Irena lives here, maybe works for him, or used to. William asks why. Marco tells him the woman stole from him, hundreds of pounds, ruined his business, went on the run. He simply wants to trace her. Then a pause. She can't see what is happening. She waits for his answer. 'Oh dear Jesus,' she whispers, pulling her clenched fist up to her mouth, pressing it against her lips.

She hears Marco. 'You understand the question I am asking you?'

'I understand,' she hears William say. Then, 'No. No one called Irena. I live alone.'

'You sure, old man? I show you a picture, just to be sure. Maybe someone like this visits you?'

Another pause.

Her eyes are closed now.

'No,' she hears him say. 'I don't know this woman.'

Another moment and Marco goes. The door is closed. Irena moves into the hall. William is still looking at the door, at the place where the man has been standing, as if an answer to something might be lying there. They say nothing, staying still, looking at each other in silence for minute after minute in case Marco is still outside or, worse, walking round the outside of the house looking in through the windows. After a while, they hear a car being driven away, but still neither of them feels safe enough to move until eventually, in silence, Irena wheels William back into the kitchen. She fills the kettle, readies the two cups. They sit drinking the tea. It is a while before either of them speaks.

'In the kitchen drawer,' he says eventually, 'to the right of the sink. There's a debit card. The pin number is 7661. Put the card in your pocket. When you go, take it. Use some of the money, all of it, I don't care. I'll never ask. The money is yours. We will never talk of this again. It's enough. To start again. Something new. You understand?'

She hesitates, then acknowledges his offer.

He is sitting at the table. She is reading to him. It is three days since the visitor in the night. Neither of them has spoken of it since. She is more careful to watch for anything unusual as she walks to and from the town. If a car slows down on the road ahead of her, she hesitates, watches it drive past. She has quit her job at the care agency. She told as many people as she dared that she had met a man and was leaving for London with him at the end of the week.

He listens to the words she reads to him. Fitzgerald. Soon, he thinks, Nick Carraway will recall Gatsby's wonder at looking out at the green light at the end of Daisy's dock.

William is tired. He thinks of the green light. He thinks of Gatsby beating on, boat against the current, borne back ceaselessly into the past. He feels a lightness. Not an unpleasant thing. A sliding. It doesn't trouble him at all. As his body edges sideways, slips down from the chair, losing gravity, he reaches out for Anna, hoping, finally, that she will catch him as he falls.

37

ALL FOUR OF US WERE in the car. We were driving along the motorway. We were going to visit a sculpture park. It was the school holidays and the sculpture park was the only place that Mum could get both Max and I to agree on. The idea of the day out been as a reward for Max, who had come third in his trials race and had been chosen to run cross country for Manchester schools. Mum asked him where he'd like us all to go. He said Chill Factor. He was, inevitably, quite good at snowboarding. I hated it. I wrote that I didn't want to go to Chill Factor. Sometimes I hated not Max exactly but the things Max could do, his accomplishments. When people described me they talked about the things I *couldn't* do. I knew it was wrong to not like Max sometimes, but then I knew I wasn't a good person. In that way I was different to Max.

'It's not your treat,' Max said.

So go stupid snowboarding, I wrote. *I'll wait in the car.*

'It's a treat for all of us,' Mum said, slightly missing the point that it was supposed to be a reward for Max coming third in some race. 'Max, where else would you like to go for the day?'

'Trafford Centre.'

'Mouse?'

No.

'Climbing wall.'

No.

'Paint balling.

No! I underlined this three times.

'What about you, Mouse? You suggest somewhere we can go.'

Jodrell Bank, I wrote. Jodrell Bank and its giant telescope was the most exciting place I could think of for a day out.

'Ugh, no,' Max said.

Finally, with Mum trying very hard, we settled on the compromise of the sculpture park.

In the days leading up to the outing, Mum won a case she hadn't expected to, and my dad announced his new research paper was going to be published in some prestigious journal, so each of these events got tacked on as extra reasons for the day out. I think that's when Mum started getting worried about me being the only one left out of this *Something to Celebrate* mood. So she made a big deal about how I had recently agreed to start seeing a new speech therapist, even though I didn't want it to be a big deal.

I'd never liked speech therapy very much. It had originally been organized by the head teacher, who'd arranged for someone to come into the school and do some tests with me. I don't think I did very well because, fairly soon after that, I had to start going to the health centre once a week for my official speech (ha ha!) therapy. The first person I saw was Mrs Ditta, who took maternity leave fairly soon after we started and after that there wasn't anyone to cover for her for a long time. I wasn't bothered because I was pretty sure that my voice had gone for good and wouldn't return. Then there was Mrs Cleary, who kept wanting to make me sing, which I hated. After that there was Miss Standish, who grew impatient within a couple of months because I hadn't started speaking as quickly as she wanted me to and she didn't seem to like me after that, which was fine because I didn't like her. That's when I wrote that I didn't want to go to any more speech therapy because I didn't mind not having a voice, and I was doing fine anyway at school. I heard Mum and Dad have an argument about it and the result was that I didn't have to go to see anyone for a while. But before my tenth birthday, Mum said we ought to have another go to give me the best chance of starting to speak again before I started secondary school. She said I didn't have to go back to the health centre, I could go to a private speech therapist. She and my dad had found a nice one and would I at least agree to meet with Sadie, please.

It's not really something you celebrate, I wrote, protesting, as the day out was being negotiated.

Mum read my note. 'Well, I think it's definitely something worth celebrating,' she said. She was wearing her brightest making-the-most-of-things expression. She said that agreeing to see Sadie on my own in her office in the city centre showed that I was growing up and why shouldn't we celebrate that?

Since I had sat on my own perfectly well with the other three speech (ha ha!) therapists at the health centre, I was unimpressed.

Can Lucas come? I wrote.

'He doesn't have to come everywhere with us,' Max said. Max was in one of his fed-up-with-Lucas phases. He had decided that Lucas wasn't always cool enough to play with.

'It's a nice idea,' Mum said, 'but maybe this time it would be nice if it was just the four of us, don't you think?'

I didn't think so.

'It's so rare we get to all go out together like this for the day,' Mum said. 'We're all usually so busy doing separate things.'

I'm not busy, I wrote in my Filofax, but I didn't even bother to tear the page out and show it to anyone. I just sat there knowing the truth was that we were going out for the day to celebrate yet another thing that Max had done. I knew that my dad would rather not be there (two nights before, me and Max had been woken by the owls again), and I knew that Max would much rather be going to Chill Factor.

I didn't know that this would be the last time the four of

us went out together as a family, that a month after our trip to the sculpture park Mum would make the decision to leave my dad for good. I know it now, but I couldn't see it then because everything only happens once and then it's gone. So on the journey I sat pretending to read a book, although actually I was mostly studying the sat nav to see how much longer we all had to sit in the car together like a happy family before I could get out at the sculpture park and go exploring on my own along the signed paths like Mum had promised me.

My dad was driving. He'd set the sat nav because we hadn't been to the sculpture park before. We were used to having it on in the car. Mum always set it, even if she knew the way. She liked to know how much of a drive was left and how long the journey would take. She liked the reminders from the voice about a turn that was coming up ahead. She said it was helpful when she was driving to court, or after a difficult day's work, not to have to think too much about where the next turn was. Max sometimes pestered Mum to get one of the celebrity voices you could buy. He thought it would be funny to have Homer Simpson giving us directions. But Mum said she liked the anonymous man's voice. It was comforting, she said, listening to his calm, unhurried instructions. She confessed that sometimes, when she missed a turn, or when she overruled the voice because she was somewhere familiar and knew a better way, she always expected the voice to get annoyed at her, the way my dad sometimes did. But the voice never got angry. It remained patient, prompting us gently towards our destination. It felt like someone watching over us, observing us making our twists and turns along the road, anticipating our next moves, knowing which way we would go. Like God.

After an hour or so on the motorway, my dad decided to turn off into the service station. He indicated and the car slowed down and moved onto the slip road. But the sat nav screen showed the car still moving along the motorway. It showed the slip road peeling off to the left, but the image of the car on the screen didn't immediately turn onto the slip road. Even as we were slowing to a dead stop near the top of the slope, preparing to turn into the car park, the sat nav was still showing the car driving steadily on down the motorway. That's what the satellites were reporting we were doing on the screen. Which, if time had stopped at that exact moment and our car had somehow vanished, is what everyone would believe the car been doing at the point when time stopped going forwards.

I read that scientists who have been exploring the far edges of the universe developed a theory that if the universe started getting smaller instead of continuing to expand it might rewind time. So if the universe had starting shrinking at that precise moment, the official records would never have shown that we had turned onto the slip road. We had been moving along the same motorway for so long that the sat nav was still assuming our direction of travel was the same.

Sadie says, 'I think we should talk about your mum.'

I think we should do speech therapy, I write.

'We haven't made much progress lately, so I thought we'd have a break from speech therapy today,' she says. 'Let's just have a catch-up. So, how's Mum doing?'

She's fine, I write up on the whiteboard.

'Still painting her landscapes?' Sadie wonders. Except Sadie never wonders anything.

I nod.

Sadie waits. She wants to see if I'm going to go stumbling into the hole up ahead that her silence has created. I realize it's possible that Sadie already knows Mum has resumed working once a week. This might be a test to see if I'm going to tell her the truth, or be caught out hiding something from her.

She's going into her office two hours a week, I write.

'Really?' Sadie says in mock surprise. 'That's good. You

must be pleased for her, Mouse.'

It's too soon, I write.

'What makes you say that?'

It just is. Maybe two hours will be all right but not any more than that.

'Are you worried for her?'

I just said – it's too soon.

'Might this have something to do with school, Mouse? This caution about your mum going back to work.'

She's only going for two hours, I write a bit crossly.

'To begin with. But then, when she increases her hours, when she gets more used to it, when she gets back into the swing...'

She's not getting back into the SWING.

I want to say Mum's still living mostly on soup, that the owls still keep her awake at night, and that it's me who makes most of our meals; that if it was up to Mum we'd probably have starved by now. I look at the whiteboard. I'm not sure what it is that made me write 'swing' in capitals. It looks more forceful than I wanted it to be. I rub the whiteboard clean in an attempt to start again.

We agreed to home education. We're staying at the farm. We like it there.

'You and your mum? You've talked about this?'

As always with Sadie, I wonder if she's fishing or if she really knows something.

Even if she works a bit more, we're still doing home education.

'Won't it get lonely up there on your own?'

I like it on my own.

'What if your mum goes back to work full time?'

She won't, I told you.

'What if she does?'

I won't get lonely. I'll be busy growing our food, so Mum only needs to work a bit.

'What about your friends? Won't they want to visit?'

What friends?

'What about Lucas?'

I told you before. We text a lot.

'But what if Lucas wants to see you? If you're not seeing him at school because you're being home educated, can he come and visit you?'

I'll be quite busy.

'Has he asked yet if he can visit you there at the farm?'

He just likes texting.

'He could help you.'

No.

'Why not?'

He doesn't text me so much any more.

'Have you guys fallen out or something?'

I think he just has other things to do.

'That's not what I heard. I'm sure he'd be happy to help.'

He couldn't help me.

'Couldn't?'

He can't come up.

I stop.

Sadie looks at what I've written. The cloth is in my hand, but I daren't rush to rub the sentence out. It's up there now. She's seen it. Sometimes it feels like Sadie has seen everything before it happens. Sometimes I worry that she can see right into me, which is very worrying. She makes out that she's reading the sentence very carefully, even though it only consists of four words. I reach across and rub it out. I feel myself tip forwards into the trap she's left for me to fall into. Too late, I realize my mistake.

Sadie waits.

I can feel a dryness in my mouth.

I lift the pen. I write it out again. *He can't come up.* I'm trying to wind back time. I'm pretending that the universe has stopped expanding, that it isn't moving relentlessly forwards. This time I leave the four words there, written on the board.

I glance across at Sadie's face for the first time in what seems like ages. She leans over and takes the pen. Beneath what I have written, she writes, *Tell me why he can't come up?*

She holds the pen out for me. I don't take it.

'Here,' Sadie says. 'Just let the pen do the writing for you, Mouse.'

I take the pen and look at it. I press it to the board. It stays in the same place for a while, and then it writes.

Because he can't.

It waits there, pressed to the whiteboard. Then it writes again.

Because of Mum.

'Tell me why because of Mum?' Sadie says. I thought she might be angry, but she's not. She leans across to me and whispers the question so softly that I can only just hear it.

Because of Max, it writes.

'Tell me why because of Max?'

Because Max died, the pen is writing.

'I know Max died,' she says. She's still whispering.

Because Lucas is a boy, the pen writes. *They were nearly the same age. He can't keep coming.*

'Why not, Mouse? It's okay. Why not?'

He'll just keep reminding Mum of Max.

'Is that what would happen, Mouse, if Lucas came to see you?'

Every time he was there she would look at him and see Max.

'And that's why Lucas has to be kept away?'

She isn't strong enough.

'How do you know that, Mouse?'

She isn't. Her son died.

'I know, Mouse.'

She isn't ever more than 4.2, and that's when she's not thinking about Max. That's why Lucas can't come.

'Does Lucas know this? Have you told him why he can't see you?'

I shake my head.

'But if she's going back to work, Mouse, does that not mean it's getting better?'

It's too soon to go to work, I write.

Sadie nods, as if she understands. 'Maybe it is,' she says. 'Maybe it is too soon.'

It is, I write.

'Maybe it is. But maybe she's not going back to work for herself, Mouse. Maybe she's going back for you.'

I don't want her to go back.

'I know you don't. But maybe she's anxious to do it for your sake. Maybe she's doing it for you. Maybe she's a tiny bit stronger than you think.'

She's not.

'Maybe she's doing this to show you that it's possible for things to change a little bit. Maybe she wants you to go to school, to make new friends. Even if it's hard for her, even if it's too soon for her to go back to work or she's not quite ready herself, maybe she's trying to make it easier for you to move on.'

I think about the car on the motorway on our way to the sculpture park the month before Max died, when we were still pretending to be an ordinary family. I think about us turning onto the slip road, slowing down, changing direction, while all the time the sat nav kept saying we were still speeding along the motorway. I think about the universe expanding and time going forwards. I wish the physicists were right and time could wind backwards. The sat nav didn't know. It hadn't yet spotted that the car had turned, that it was going somewhere else. Our direction of travel had been the same constant for so long that it didn't anticipate that the car might have changed direction.

I realize that, in the same way, I'm not sure any more where my life with Mum is going and whether, without me noticing, it may already have changed direction.

38

My dear girl,

I wish you could have seen the spectacle. Two thousand officers, many of them in dress uniform, some wearing medals from the civil war, from the tsar, gathered together in the barracks square in the sunshine, ready to leave the camp to meet with the British field marshal that afternoon.

Around the square, their families had gathered to see them off. Some of them, it is true, were cautious, upset. One or two were even crying through fear and uncertainty. Anna had been readying Vasilenko in his dress uniform. He had brushed aside her puzzlement about why it was necessary for two thousand men to be bussed across the valley to meet with one field marshal rather than have Alexander come to meet them here. He told her that he trusted the British. He had reassured his field officers when he had made his telephone calls the previous evening. General Domanov had already set off for the conference from his HQ in Lienz. Vasilenko told Anna not to fret, that he would be back between six and eight that evening. He kissed her on the forehead before climbing into the Fiat for the ride to Oberdrauburg a dozen miles away. She came to tell me this. She seemed finally reassured. She embraced me, for the first time unconcerned about openly showing her affection for me. A line of sixty trucks, each one filled with officers, followed the Fiat out of the compound, taking the salutes of old men, young boys, widows, mothers, all of them lining the roadside. In the square the departing trucks threw up a haze of dust that hung in the air for a long time after they were gone.

Only when the last truck was out of sight was I taken to one side and asked to report to the major at HQ. He told me that there was no conference at Oberdrauburg, or anywhere else. There was to be no British Foreign Legion, no Italian enclave. Out of sight of the camp, the convoy had been flanked by a contingent of British armoured cars and armed motorcycle outriders. The Cossack officers were being taken to the Soviet zonal frontier at Judenburg, to be handed over to the Red Army.

39

Why dark matter can't be seen if there's so much of it
How some things are so far away that, by the time you see them, they have ceased to exist
How a forgiveness machine works

'I DID SOME HOMEWORK,' Sadie says, 'about the Andromeda galaxy.'

You said you weren't interested in stars, I write.

'I got persuaded,' she says, shrugging. 'Someone persuaded me. I got some book tokens for my birthday and I bought a book about astronomy and stuff.'

It was your birthday?

'Sure, even speech therapists have birthdays. And I realized I didn't want you keeping all this good stuff to yourself.'

You told me you were only interested in people.

'Yes, but then something kept nagging me, you know. You kept dropping these hints to me about how it was so cool, all this looking up at this enormous universe, all this searching for stars and galaxies and stuff. And then when I started reading a bit about it, I finally got it. The book kept talking about how big the whole place is, and how long it would take to get anywhere in the universe, however fast you travelled. I realized that looking up at the stars turns us into time travellers, which is secretly what I always wanted to do when I was little.'

You wanted to time travel? I write.

'I still would. Wouldn't that be so cool, to go time travelling? So then I read this thing about the Andromeda galaxy. That's a place that's like the same size as our Milky Way.'

I know! I write.

'Turns out that the universe is so enormous that, when the light we can see today from the Andromeda galaxy set off on its journey to reach Earth, travelling at all those gazillions of miles an hour, human beings didn't exist.'

186,000, I write.

'That's right,' Sadie says, as if I've jogged her memory. 'One hundred and eighty-six thousand miles a second. And the time it took for the light from Andromeda to arrive at the Earth was twenty-five million, million, million years. And you've been keeping all this good stuff from me, Mouse de Bruin.'

They took a photograph from the Hubble space station, I write. *It has a hundred billion lights on it.*

'And each of the lights is a star?' Sadie asks.

No, each of the lights is a galaxy.

Sadie's head seems to swirl at the thought of it.

I tell her, *The photograph has red galaxies on it that are at the edge of the universe.*

'Why red?' she asks.

Red light has been stretched the most, I tell her. *It means the space between those galaxies and us has stretched the most. Which means our universe is getting bigger.*

'Why's it getting bigger?' she says.

Why do you sometimes ask questions when you know the answer? I write.

'Do I know the answer?'

You said you read a book, I write. *It must have told you about the Big Bang, so you must already know the answer.*

'Yes,' she says. 'The Big Bang.'

Before the Big Bang, our universe was smaller than a grain of sand.

'Now do you want to tell me that's not interesting, Mouse de Bruin?'

I know it's interesting.

'You've kept it from me all these months, but now I'm hooked.' She smiles, pretending to be exasperated.

I didn't keep anything from you!

'You didn't tell me hard enough. You told me you had a telescope and you looked at the stars, but you didn't tell me how amazing it was to do that.'

Yes I did.

'Well, you didn't tell me hard enough.'

You didn't ask me enough.

'But I suppose you got me there in the end, didn't you? That's what a good teacher does, I guess. Excites your curiosity. Leaves you wanting to find out more.'

My work here is done? I write.

'Pretty much,' she says, teasing me. 'I'll think of it as your gift to me. Something I can enjoy long after you and I have stopped meeting up like this.'

Don't mention it, I write. *I'll send my bill.*

'So, who got you your telescope?'

And it's as if the smoothly driven car I'm sitting in has lurched into an unexpected gear. The flow of our conversation slams to a halt as I try to work out how to reverse out of the mess I'm in. Finally I write, *You know who did.*

'Do I?'

Yes.

'Was it your dad?'

I shrug.

Sadie nods, as though she didn't know, but she did. 'What was it, a birthday present?'

Yes.

'How old were you? Six, seven?'

Six.

'Is your dad interested in space? In astronomy?'

It's his job.

'What does he do?'

He works at the university. You know this stuff. I know you do.

'People tell me so many things, Mouse, I can't remember them all.'

You don't forget anything.

'So remind me what he does.'

He's a physicist.

'And he taught you all this stuff, about the Hubble telescope and everything?'

I learned it myself. Most of it. I read books. I like finding things out.

'About the universe? About the stars?'

Yes.

'And it was your dad who got you going? Sparked your interest?'

You said yourself, it's interesting.

'And that's what you two used to do together?'

Sometimes.

'You went to Jodrell Bank? Did things like that together?'

I don't answer her.

'That's a good thing for a father to give to a daughter, don't you think, Mouse de Bruin? That passion for something?'

And then I write, *I don't want to talk about my dad.*

'Why not, Mouse?'

It won't work, I write.

'What won't? Tell me what won't work.'

It won't work trying to get me to like him.

'Who says I want you to like him?'

All this stuff about pretending to like astronomy and about him buying me the telescope.

'Is that not true, about the telescope, about him teaching you about the planets?'

So what?

'So maybe it's not as black and white as it sometimes seems. That's all I'm saying, Mouse. I mean, I know things didn't work out between him and your mum, but maybe it's possible that your dad isn't all completely bad. Maybe he did some good things as well. Even your mum must have loved your dad at one time for them to get married, mustn't she?'

No.

'No?'

I lift the pen and underline the word twice.

'No, she didn't love him?'

I don't reply.

'Or no, she doesn't any more? Tell me, Mouse.'

NO, I write again beneath it.

'No to what, Mouse?'

No we're not moving back in with him.

'Is that what you think I want, Mouse? For you and your mum to move back in with your dad?'

You want me to think good things about him.

'And if you say good things about your dad, then it might happen? Is that what you're worried about?'

Stop trying to make me say good things.

'I'm not trying to make you say anything. Really, Mouse, I'm not.'

STOP IT. STOP IT.

'Mouse? Are you all right?'

I want a toilet break.

'Right now?'

I want one.

I don't wait for an answer, even though I know I'm breaking the rules, all three of them. Sadie's Golden Rules. Tell the Truth; Always Get Permission from the Other Person before Breaking off from a Session; Respect Each Other.

I stand up and leave the room and go down the corridor, pushing past someone coming the other way whom I don't really see very well because of the watery film over my eyes. It's hard to breathe, and the air in my chest gets snagged like some griping hiccup that won't quite come out. It builds and builds, swelling behind my ribcage and I push open the door to the Ladies, and only when the door swings closed behind me does the pressure burst like a sob.

I'm six years old. I'm downstairs in the utility room. There's a party up above me in the house. The party is to celebrate the fact that my dad's book has just been published. Before the book came out, two people from different newspapers came to interview him.

People are happy. Max is pretending to be the DJ. I'm lying snugly in the big laundry cupboard on my hammock of clean white towels reading *The Tiger Who Came to Tea*.

It's warm in the utility room. The central heating boiler is down here, and the washer and the dryer. It's my favourite place in the house, especially if the washing machine or the dryer is running and its background hum is soaking up all the other noises and makes it feel like a small, separate world of its own.

We use the room to store our walking coats and outdoor boots, and Max's sports equipment. Along with the washer and dryer, it leaves just enough room for an old red leather armchair in the corner by the door, which has to be moved whenever someone wants to go out of the side of the house that way. The armchair is the other good place to sit and read down here. My parents say the chair must never be thrown away. They bought it in a junk shop and had it in their first tiny flat when they were students and they can't bear to throw it out, even though it sometimes gets in the way and Max is always leaving his coats or muddy kit draped over it. It's in the way, Max says. Can't we get rid of it? We're saving it, my dad always says, for when we get a bigger house with a library or a study where the chair can finally live in a happy-ever-after kind of way. Sometimes Mum finds me asleep in the laundry cupboard down here and sweeps me up in one of the bath towels and, carrying me over to the chair, she cuddles me. You're like a little mouse, squished up in here, she says.

I like that it's a small space in the laundry cupboard. I like the sense that I'm a small animal burrowing deep down in a place that no one else in the world has discovered.

I usually leave the door open just enough to let in some light to read by. Sometimes, if it's full, I have to take a couple of towels out so there's enough room for me to nestle down comfortably in there and turn the pages of my book without my elbow catching the door and pushing it too far open. When Mum has just washed a bunch of towels and they've been stacked in the laundry cupboard, the warmth still drifting from them smells like bread rising.

Upstairs at the party, I kept wandering into draughts from open doors where people were perched half in and half out of the house with their cigarettes. The smokers were supposed to be out in the garden or on the drive, but it's raining and the wind is cold. Those who weren't smoking were drinking and laughing. Some of them had started dancing to the music that was playing. Mum was laughing, too, in her jeans and the new blue top that she went shopping for in the city. I would have liked a cuddle, but she was busy moving in and out of the kitchen to check on the food, and topping up the wine and beer in people's glasses. People were mostly talking about boring things, about colleagues they work with who were stupid or stupid rules they had to follow. One or two of Mum's friends from her firm are here, but it's mainly my dad's colleagues – other lecturers at the university, faculty staff, the two researchers who work for him and who live together, Kyra and Rolf – Kyra in a thin, filmy dress that seems to float around her and Rolf in his ridiculous trendy T-shirt and beret. All of them, of course, know a ton of stuff about the universe, and all of them fell straight away in love with Max, who is eight and a half and who is fizzing round the house like a firework. He doesn't get tongue-tied like me.

People upstairs wanted to know if we were rich yet because of my dad's book. I wasn't sure if they were teasing us or not.

They asked what kind of house we were going to buy. They laughed about whether my dad would change when he was famous. Max joined in and said when we were rich he was going to have a recording studio and an indoor swimming pool. My dad smiled with that look on his face that Mum calls 'goofy', as though people had got the wrong man, like it could never happen to him. When Max finished telling them about his saxophone and athletics and swimming, people turned to me and tousled my hair and asked me what I was good at doing. Each time, I tried to think of a smart reply but the words flew out of my head and I was left looking solemn and serious when I really didn't want to be. At one point my dad joined in and said that I was going to be an astronomer. He explained about the telescope he had bought me for my birthday. He gave me one of his winks and I found a way of slipping away to my hideaway down here.

I'm snuggled inside the cupboard on my layers of towels. All the grown-ups are having the kind of good time that I'm not so good at having. Poor Mouse, Mum would say if she found me here, but Mum is busy making sure everyone else is having fun. I can hear the music boom-booming upstairs across the two lounges, the hallway, the kitchen and the conservatory, although the laundry cupboard muffles the sound of the music nicely, as if it's all slightly underwater. Only the voices in the back hall are clear enough for me to hear. At one point, I hear two or three people gather there, taking turns to try to blow a note on Max's saxophone. I listen to Max collapse in fits of giggles at their failed attempts. Later, I hear my dad and Mum talking as they pass through together. He wonders if I should be in bed; she says to give me a little longer, says it's good for me to be around people like this. It's a special night, she says. Their voices move away. I feel pleased that they aren't coming looking for me yet. That's because some guests, who have travelled up from London for the party, are staying over tonight and they are using my bedroom. I'm sharing Max's room with him and I know I won't get to sleep for ages in there, what with all those posters of cyborgs and wrestlers. I settle like a bird in my nest of towels and read about the Tiger one more time. He politely drinks the house dry, thanks Sophie and her mum and then departs, and even though the family buy in a tin of tiger food, he never comes again. I fall asleep.

A small noise wakes me. It might be five minutes later, or an hour – I can't tell. The thud of music upstairs sound just the same. The arm that I fell asleep on has gone numb. I lie very still. Footsteps come down the six steps. I hear two hushed voices, giggling. I can't see who it is. From where my head has settled in the laundry cupboard I only have a view of the old red leather armchair in the corner through the gap in the slightly open door. There is a flutter of fabric close to me, something floaty. I recognize the dress. It's Kyra, the research assistant. I wait for Rolf to slip into view with his ridiculous beret. She says something to him. But when the figure appears, it isn't Rolf. It's my dad. He is holding a glass of wine.

'Over there,' she says in a way I haven't heard her talk before, gesturing to the leather chair. In one hand, she too is holding wine; in the other hand is a key.

'Is it locked?' he whispers.

I watch Kyra hold up the key between her forefinger and thumb. My dad moves over to the chair as he is told. Kyra shakes her hair. The filmy dress that she is wearing ripples. She stands in front of him. She says something to him in a whisper that I can't hear. He laughs. I see him wriggle about in the chair. She kneels over him, then straddles him, letting her dress ride up her legs. She settles in her position. He has his goofy face on. I see him smiling, looking up at her. He reaches out with his free hand and lifts one shoulder strap of the dress off her shoulder. I see her breast. My dad puts his hand on it. Kyra starts to move slowly up and down. A small animal sound comes out of my dad's mouth. Kyra stops moving and says something to him that I can't hear. His eyes close and she laughs like something is funny. She starts to rise and fall again in her funny squatting position, gently at first and then a little faster and a little faster, until he makes a sudden lurch like electricity has flooded into him that makes him gasp out loud.

'Fuck,' he says. 'My fucking lord.'

'That's for being such a clever boy,' she says.

They laugh together.

He slides one hand across her bottom through the flow of her dress.

'We should go back,' she says. 'Bloody Rolf will be wanting to bore you again.'

'I know,' he says. 'I know.'

She slips from his lap and straightens her dress. He stands up. For the first time I see that his trousers were round his knees. She kisses him. In that moment, the elbow I have moved a fraction, in an effort to stop the pins and needles getting worse, brushes very lightly against the laundry cupboard door. It swings slowly halfway out in its arc, and stops. The two of them look round and see me for the first time.

He says, 'Oh, sh—' and stops himself.

'I think she's been asleep,' Kyra whispers.

There is a second's pause. Then my dad brings the forefinger of his right hand to his lips and makes a 'Sshh' sign at me, like he needs us both to be quiet. And then he winks at me like he sometimes does, as if to say that everything is fine, that there's nothing here for me to worry about, and they turn and are gone, back up the stairs.

40

My dear girl,

It becomes hard to speak of such things. That evening I asked to be relieved from my duties as liaison officer to the camp. The major listened to my request, and then refused. I asked what was to happen to the Cossack population, now without their officers. He said that all the Cossacks were to be handed over to the Red Army. This had been the Russians' request, and the British had agreed to it. I asked if that included women and children. He said yes. I said I didn't think I would be able to carry out such an action. He grew short with me. He gave me a direct order. He said to refuse would mean a court martial.

I went in search of Anna. By now, people in the camp knew that their officers were several hours overdue. Rumours were everywhere. Each time someone stopped me and asked about them I said I didn't know where they were. Each time I was asked, I stopped short of saying they would be returning to the camp. In my head I had started to formulate plans for how I could smuggle Anna, and the boy too, if need be, out of the camp. I could drive her out in the jeep, get her back over the border into Italy. I could organize papers for her. I could turn her into an Austrian or an Italian. I searched everywhere I could think of in the town, the barracks, around the valley, until it grew dark, but I could find no trace of her. Everybody I asked claimed not to have seen her since the afternoon. I had seen no sign of the boy, either, and I began to think that perhaps she had learned of the officers' fate and taken it upon herself to flee into the mountains with the boy. I slept little that night.

The next morning, I was ordered to go to the hotel that had been General Domanov's headquarters, where the wives of the officers had gathered. My job was to tell them what had happened to their husbands and to confirm that the women would soon be joining them. I took half a dozen men with me to ensure order was maintained. Soon after I started to speak women began to cry. I told them they were to organize their husbands' belongings, which would be forwarded to them. I said they could write letters. I said arrangements were being made for the wives to join them in the next few days, that we would endeavour to make sure that everyone was well treated. Someone screamed. One elderly woman fainted. Some started shouting. Raising my voice, I said the only thing I could, that I was obeying orders. I returned to the hotel later in the day to oversee the transfer of the officers' luggage. The place was deserted. The wives had gone down to the barracks at Peggetz a mile away to be with their countrymen. In the ballroom they had left behind a series of neatly organized sacks and wooden crates, each one labelled with the name of the Cossack officer whose personal effects it contained. On the top of many of them were letters written to husbands or sons. I inspected some of them, then I sat down on the step that led up to the raised stage at the front of the ballroom where, before the war, some prim little Austrian orchestra would have played for guests to dance to after supper. I was waiting for the two lorries to arrive, which were to collect the luggage. I sat there for a while in something of a trance. And then I looked up and saw her in the doorway. I felt a tremor run through me. She had already seen me. She looked across at me. I watched her walk half the length of the ballroom and stop, with enough deliberation to show that she would come no further.

My Anna. My world.

She spoke. 'Do you know what you've done?' she asked.

I made half a step towards her.

'It's a death sentence,' she said. Her voice spilled round the high-ceilinged room and died. I stopped in my tracks.

'The Russians are our allies,' I told her. 'They fought with us against the Nazis. And Cossacks are Russians.'

'You know what will happen to the letters in this room, to the clothes, the uniforms, the photographs? They will put them in a pile at Judenburg and pour petrol on them and throw a lighted rag into the middle.'

'You can't be sure of that, Anna. I'm told they…'

'You want to know what happened to our officers? You want to know in what ways some of them tried to kill themselves when they realized they were to be handed over? I can tell you about the officer who took a razor to his throat in front of the British who were assembling them at the bridge.'

'Anna, please…'

'You want to hear about Dimitri Sukalo? As if Stalin's men had not already done enough to him. You know that he asked at the bridge at Judenburg to be let off the truck to urinate and ran to the edge of the bridge and leaped over. You know what they did, your comrades? They dragged him, dying, from the rocks in the ravine a hundred feet below to present him to the Russians. I think, perhaps, the British must getting paid for every Cossack they hand over to Stalin's thugs.'

'You don't know this. Any of this.'

'You think? You think I don't know? I tell you I sat with a captain, Belozersky, today. He escaped with two others from one of the trucks as it approached the bridge at Judenburg. The other two were shot by your friends, but Belozersky escaped into the woods. He waited for cover of darkness to make his way back here to warn people, his family, anyone who would believe him. He hid in the hills and saw what happened. After the handover he heard gunfire in the steel mill across the river where the Russians had taken them. Lots of shots. Sometimes machine guns. He heard the screams. You should be proud, Captain Crosby. Stalin and Beria will be well pleased with you for doing their dirty work.'

I think, by now, I had started to weep. I would like to say it was for the Cossacks, for those officers who had already perished, for what might lie ahead. But, in truth, I was crying, I think, for my own loss, for this woman, who had saved my life, who was now my implacable foe.

'I can save you,' I said, from somewhere in the choke of tears. 'Anna, I can get you out. Please.'

'I am a Cossack, remember. Only fit for selling to the Russians.'

'I can buy a passport, papers. Italian, Greek, anything. We can live in England. I can get you out tonight.'

'You would have me leave the boy?'

'We can take the boy.'

'And what about the colonel? And Dmitri Sukalo? Are we to ask the Russians to hand them back? Maybe Sukalo in pieces? You think, Captain, huh? Are we taking them with us too, over the mountains, to England? Maybe you can turn them into Englishmen, or Italians? And what about all the wives of the officers you lied to today?'

'I didn't lie.'

'You didn't lie when you said they could join their husbands? That families would be kept together? Where? In a Siberian labour camp? In a cell in the Lubyanka? In the river at Judenburg?'

And then something made her move towards me.

'Did you know?' she asked, as though the thought had suddenly occurred to her. 'Did you know all this was going to happen? All the time we were together? At the villa? Did you know?'

She stepped closer again.

'Anna, I swear to you I didn't. I didn't know.'

She stopped in front of me.

'I didn't know,' I repeated. It was all I could manage to say. I wanted to reach out and hold her. I wanted so much to weep in her arms. I stepped down onto the ballroom floor to stand alongside her. I suddenly thought of the people who had danced together on this floor in years gone by to Hoagy Carmichael, to Cole Porter.

'How can I believe you?' she said.

'Anna, you have to believe what I say. It was an order. Suddenly, an order.'

'From the field marshal with whom you have tea?' The same words she had once used warmly, teasingly, were spat out now.

'It's not too late to get you out, Anna. Please let me help you.'

'I don't believe you. I don't believe anything any more the British say to me.' She leaned away from me, as if preparing to turn away, and then her arm came out and struck me a blow in the chest, and then three or four other blows followed. I did nothing to protect myself. I left my hands by my side. She hit me on the side of my face with her small, clenched fist, too quickly for me to react. She caught me on the lip. I felt the small burst of flesh as she did so, like the segment of an orange splitting.

41

'I FELT THE SMALL BURST OF FLESH as she did so, like the segment of an orange splitting. I put my finger to the blood on my lip. She didn't look at me. She looked at her small fist, then she turned away from me and walked slowly back across the ballroom and out of the hotel. She didn't look back. The door made no sound as she closed it.

'You must see, my dear girl, you must believe. I didn't know. I didn't know. Your mother did not believe me. I cannot blame her for that. I ask only that you find it possible, one day, to believe it is the truth. So, enough for now. Enough. I am so tired. I will write again soon, my love. I promise. My fondest wishes to you. William.'

I turn the last page of the letter over and lay it down on the bed. William's hand is resting free beside it. There is the smallest twitch in his fingers. I see them raise a fraction and then subside. I sit waiting, hoping, for another sign of movement, a slow gathering of his senses, but there is none. He lies still in his bed again. Then something makes me glance round. Alice is standing behind me in the doorway. I don't know how long she has been there.

'You read very well,' she says.

For a moment I think she can see inside my head. Then I realize she has been listening.

Then I realize I must have been reading out loud.

◆ ◆ ◆

After the night of the party, some things changed. For one, I never went back to read in the laundry cupboard. Instead, I started to make my dens with sheets draped over two dining chairs in front of the big bay window and listened, as I read silently, to the rain spit against the window. For another, my dad got rid of the red leather armchair he had been storing down in the utility room, claiming it was finally going mouldy.

A year later, Mum left my dad for the first time, taking me and Max with her away from the avenue. Three weeks after that, we went back again. My dad assured her that the woman he'd slept with had been the only one. Her name was Erin and she was on the faculty staff at the university. He said it was a dreadful mistake he had made and he regretted it. He asked Mum to bring us back home. Max, I think, was simply glad to move back into his room with his posters and his saxophone, back to his schedule of activities and his friends. I remember how happy Mum was, too. I know how much she loved my dad.

On our first night back on the avenue, Mum served tea and said wasn't it a good thing we were all back together again, and my dad, as she turned to spoon the vegetables in the dish, put his finger to his lips and smiled at me as if to say that everything was fine now, wasn't it. He suggested that we should get a dog. He said it would be good for us to have something we could all share an interest in together.

I never told Mum about Kyra. I should have done. I couldn't find a way. I tried and tried, but I heard her keep saying how, in a way, it had been her fault. She had put herself on trial, considered the evidence and pronounced herself as guilty as my dad for not working hard enough at their marriage. I heard her say to my dad that she was going to try harder, that she didn't want to ruin all our lives for the sake of one mistake. But I knew there was a lie here. I knew there wasn't just Erin. I knew about Kyra, but there was never any mention of Kyra from either of them.

I didn't tell her, even though I should have done, and so we went back to the avenue, but later on it turned out there was another woman with a different name, and after that the owls began to keep us awake, and so Mum left the house with us a second time late one evening, with half an hour's worth of belongings crushed into the car, except that this time, driving when she was angry and crying, Mum went through a junction on green on the flyover and a white van, crashing the red, struck us a glancing blow that flipped us onto our roof like we were a stunt car and our car stopped much more quickly than the front seat passenger it was carrying.

Mum was very sure that Max's death in the crash that second time she left my dad was all her fault. That's the problem if you don't have all the facts at your disposal. You end up, like my dad would say to his students, with a faulty proposition. You need more data. Like knowing how much of it I was to blame for. Like knowing that, if I'd told her about my dad and Kyra kissing and stuff at the party when I should have done the first time she left him, Max would still be alive. But long before then my body had started to run out of words. They had all flown out of me, like birds migrating to a distant land.

The sunshine makes the outskirts of the city dusty. The carriage of the Metro tram I'm in, riding back to the city centre, is striped with lines of shade and sun. I want to text 266 to explain about what happened with my voice in William's room. I start with something easier. I announce that I've taken a J. D. Salinger book of short stories out of the library. Within a couple of minutes I get a response that says, *Good, I hope you enjoy it. Give it time.*

Someone I know is dying, I text. *I've just been to see him. He's very old.*

I get another response. *That must be difficult for you.*

I text: *I wanted to tell him things, but it's too late now. So I just sit with him. Alice said that was enough.*

Who's Alice?

One of the nurses.

Does it help?

Yes. But I wish I'd known him better. Did you ever think that about someone who was dying?

In the city centre the tram glides past people who walk along in shirtsleeves, who sit at pavement tables outside cafés with the heat on their backs and the blue sky stretched above the city's roofs.

There's still twenty minutes before I'm due to meet up with Mum for the tram ride back to Bury where our car is parked. I decide to go to the coffee house to order a take out from Pavel with my voice. I want to see if it will work in public, in the open city. The idea of my having a voice is as unexpected as the sunshine.

The tram passes the entrance to Sadie's office block. I scrutinize the lobby to see if Sadie is coming or going, but the woman pushing open the door to leave the building isn't Sadie – it's Mum. She glances either side of her. She holds open the door for someone else. He passes through. It's my dad. They stand together on the pavement, as close as an embrace. The tram keeps moving forward and then I lose sight of them.

42

My dear girl,

I must tell you of the final morning. I can avoid it no longer. When I arrived in the barracks square, the priests were saying Mass. The congregation was like a city in itself. There were four, maybe five thousand of them gathered there.

We had given two days' notice to the camp's inhabitants of what we mockingly referred to as the repatriation. With the camp now having no officers, no arms or ammunition, someone had decided that the best way to get this thing done was to give them notice to prepare.

They used the two days, led principally I believe by Anna, to organize what protests they could. They hung black flags. They created placards. BETTER DEATH HERE THAN OUR SENDING INTO SSSR. Another said, WE ARE NOT SOVIET CITIZENS. They refused to eat the food which was still being distributed around the camp. The soldiers left it in piles and drove off. The Cossacks fixed black flags on poles into the mounds of food. Some of them shot their animals. When I went on my rounds, as I was still compelled to do, I saw horses lying in the fields. Men and women, as I walked past, pushed passports into my face proving they were citizens of half a dozen other countries. They were French, Yugoslav, Italian, or émigrés who had fled Russia after the revolution. I'm obeying orders, is all I could say. I could only plead with them to co-operate with us. One old woman stood in front of me and held out her hands. Each of her fingers had no nail in the bed. 'Stalin!' she said. I turned away.

A petition had been drawn up, proclaiming that the entire Cossack population in the valley preferred death at the hands of the British rather than being sent to Soviet Russia, and it was handed in to the brigade's HQ in the town. I was given other petitions, too, on my route around the camp, addressed to Winston Churchill, to the king, the Pope. I took them. In return, I passed on notes addressed to Anna to people who knew her, pleading with her to contact me. When I asked if any of them knew where she was, they would not answer.

For a while I watched the priests in their vestments saying their Mass in the square, determined to give them this at least. Several officers, including Brody, each led assignments of half a dozen men from the brigade around the edge of the square ready to usher people into the lorries.

But the deadline passed, and it became clear they were set on continuing their worship. It was, I suppose, the only protest left open to them. I had no option. Under the gaze of the major, who stood observing from his jeep at the entrance to the barracks, I had one of the interpreters issue an instruction through a megaphone for the service to draw to a close within ten minutes and after that people should start boarding the trucks that were standing by. When the ten minutes had passed and the service still continued, I gave them a further five minutes. Their prayers continued. At that point, I was ordered by the major to organize the advance on the congregation and start to force people into the lorries.

How does an army fight against an unarmed crowd composed largely of women and children? I gave an instruction for Brody's contingent to move forward carefully to cut off one small section of the crowd from the rest. I thought that if I could get the first truck filled in this way then the rest of the crowd might relent and begin to go voluntarily. The troops managed to split a group of about two hundred and herd them into one corner of the square, but as the men advanced, the cornered group began to link arms. It was then I saw that Anna was among them, with the boy next to her. Both of them had their arms linked with the people on either side of them. The troops moved to within a few paces of them. The Cossacks, seemingly on a command from Anna, kneeled down together on the ground, their arms still linked tightly together. They were singing a hymn, their faces pressed down into the dirt. Soldiers started to prise individuals apart from the huddled group and carry or drag them one by one towards the first of the lorries, which were waiting to speed them out of the camp the few hundred yards to the train which I knew was standing by with its fifty cattle wagons, their windows barred. Men and women wrestled to avoid being separated from the rest of the group. One of the soldiers under Brody's command grasped an old man by the shoulders and then suddenly reeled away holding out his hand where he had been bitten and blood had been drawn. The soldier turned back towards the man on the ground. He raised the butt of his rifle and struck hard at the man's head.

43

Where light goes inside a black hole
Stopping slugs from eating lettuces
Why Sadie is lying

I HAVEN'T TOLD SADIE ABOUT reading William's letters out loud. I haven't told anyone. Only Alice at the nursing home, and William, if he can hear me, know about my voice returning.

Sadie says, 'I think we ought to try another supervised contact with your dad.'

No.

'Mouse, do you think it's possible he might have recognized that he did some things wrong?'

He did do things wrong.

'I know that, Mouse. But just because someone knows how long it takes for light to get to Earth from Andromeda doesn't mean he knows how to talk to his daughter. About the dumb things he did, and the dumb way he handled it.'

I don't care.

'Mouse, grown-ups make mistakes. Most of us know lots about a tiny little pile of things and not much about the rest of life. Look at me. I only know one thing about the universe, about how far away Andromeda is. That's why I'm a speech therapist and not a physicist.'

I have the pen in my hand. I think about how people in the Andromeda galaxy wouldn't find out about how Max stopped much more slowly than the car he was in for twenty-five million, million, million years. I think about the way the white van touched the side of our car on the flyover, the way we flipped into the air like we had practised the stunt for months. I think about the promise I made to Mum to stay the course with Sadie. I think about Sadie's Three Golden Rules. I put my pen to the whiteboard.

You're not a speech therapist, I write.

Sadie looks at me, measuring what I've written for half a nanosecond longer than she would normally do.

'Am I not?' she says.

You know you're not.

'What am I, Mouse?'

You're a psychologist.

'What makes you say that?'

Because that's what your website says.

Sadie nods, as if on this one she may be beaten.

Because I may be a stupid little mouse, but I know how to look on people's websites.

'I'm still here to help you speak, Mouse. That's still my job.'

No it's not. It's because people think I'm stupid and that's why I can't speak.

'No one ever said you were stupid, Mouse. Is that what you think?'

What about your three golden rules?

'What about them?'

You broke them all. You didn't tell the truth. You lied to me.

'I didn't lie, Mouse. That's not what I'm here to do.'

Does Mum come here?

'I'm sorry?'

I point to the question again, jabbing the whiteboard with the pen where dots are being made one by one like a swarm of ants. My mouth is pinched shut. I'm breathing quickly. My neck is so tense that it is aching.

'Why are you asking me, Mouse?'

I can feel Sadie wriggling just like I've had to do for all these months. I can see her edging round her Three Golden Rules when, in reality, she smashed them into pieces on my first day here.

I saw her, I write.

'Mouse, what did you see?'

She said she was going to work but she was coming here.

'She came here to talk, Mouse. That was all.'

Does my dad come here?

'Mouse, tell me what you saw.'

Are you trying to get them back together?

'Mouse, that's not my job.'

You're lying again.

'No, Mouse.'

You're always lying.

'Mouse, please. Don't go. Let's talk.'

I don't want to come back here again.

'Please, Mouse. We've got this wrong, I know. I'm so sorry.' Briefly she puts her head in her hands.

Mum drives me home. My breaths are still quick and shallow. I sit in the front passenger seat. I'm not bothered this time if the car stops quicker than I do. I don't care any more. The ridiculous warmth of the day persists. I'm too hot, sat in my coat. I can feel the heat in my face. Mum knows that something has happened in my session with Sadie, I can tell by her expression. But she doesn't ask me. She just smiles. I don't ask if Sadie has rung her on her mobile. I haven't asked if she and my dad are getting back together. No one tells the truth any more.

As we turn into the drive, she announces, 'I have a surprise for you at the house.'

That's all she says. I don't ask her what she means. I get out of the car and we walk towards the house together.

'You know how much I love you, Mouse,' she says. 'How

much I want things to be right. Need them to be.'

I'm not sure what she's telling me, this person who is meeting Sadie secretly, who I'm pretty sure now is planning with my dad to move back in with him when she knows that is the wrong thing to do. I push open the door and step inside the kitchen. The figure sitting there at the big table turns towards me. It's not my dad.

It's so much worse.

I stand there in the doorway with a physical feeling in my head like gravity is collapsing. I turn to Mum as a million, million rules I had set up to protect us both are smashed to pieces, while Lucas, pale, blinking, still in his coat, sitting upright with his thin hands resting on the table, is waiting patiently for me to acknowledge his presence in the room.

But I can't.

He mustn't be here. He mustn't know. Lucas must believe we live in London. That's the only way it can be.

I open my mouth to speak.

No words come out. I'm starting to breathe fast, but somehow the air isn't reaching my lungs. I turn towards Mum and confront her about what she's done. From my tightening throat comes a sound like the scratch of a violin string, rising and falling. I'm shouting now, in these words like violin scrapes, that we can't have Lucas back in our lives because every single time Mum sees Lucas she will also be forced to see Max, and if that happens I know she'll never get better. And every time I see Lucas I'll have to think about Max, and then I'll remember each time that it's my fault that Max died, that if I'd told Mum about Kyra when I should have done Max would still be alive. If I'd told her, then Mum wouldn't have given my dad another chance and we wouldn't have been in the car crash when we left him for the second time. That's why I can't have Lucas as a friend any more, I yell at her. That's why he can't know where we are. Can't she see? Can't she see this? My shouting gives off heat and light but no words that carry any meaning.

Mum looks so pale as I try to force words out, but I don't care any more. She tries to tell me to calm down, to think about Lucas who sits there, owl-faced, saying nothing because there is nothing he can say. Come and sit down, she pleads, but I can't be stopped now, and my rage forces out tears in place of the words that, no matter how much I try, will not come. Mum moves towards me, tries to hug me, but I break away from her and turn and run from the room, out of the door, outside, round the side of the house into the walled garden, which is bathed in sunshine. I look at the rows of vegetables in William's soil that I've planted so we can stay here for ever. We don't need them now. There's no point, any more, trying to keep the world at bay. No need for broad beans and potatoes. No need for watchtowers or walls. Our defences have been breached. I go into the outhouse, searching for something to grab hold of. I see the saxophone cupped in its stand. I grasp it in both hands, carry it out into the garden. I wield it like a bat. I hit out at stalks, at lines of cabbages, at frames of climbing beans. I swing blows into the raised beds, crushing rows of salad leaves and clusters of herbs. I aim another blow and this time I misjudge the distance. The saxophone clatters into the stone of the raised bed and I feel it buckle. I hurl it to the ground and don't look back. I run on, through the gate, across the paddock, down the field. I pick up speed, coat flapping, running harder. I look ahead of me and see Anthony, draped over the fence with his long man-boy's arms. He glances up, alarmed, and sees me flying down the hill at him. I find a breath inside me that releases air and then a noise comes from me like a river's rush, a howl. The man-boy turns in terror as I run straight at him, turns and stumbles as he tries to flee, one leg trapped behind the other and he falls as if my roar has knocked him to the ground. I climb the fence and run again, as if the world is ending.

44

My dear girl,

It was the fear that drove them back.

As the first of them were ripped from the pack, clubbed if necessary and carried across to the waiting truck, the remaining huddle began to back away, towards the sanctuary of the larger mass from whom they had been separated in the square. The tightly knit group began to splinter. People began to run, but there was nowhere to run to. The crush was terrible. People shoved in any direction to avoid being trampled or suffocated. Soldiers grabbed hold of the legs or arms of children as mothers fought to hold on to them. People fell to the ground with blood flowing from head wounds inflicted by rifle butts or clubs. The altar was knocked over, the vestments of the priests were ripped as people struggled to escape, soldiers struck out, and the body of Cossacks was driven back towards the fence running alongside the river.

And then I caught sight of Anna again, this time with her back to the fence, where the post had buckled against the pressure of the swaying crowd. I saw her grasp the boy and give him an instruction above the screams and the chaos around her. I watched her shove him underneath the fence, exhorting him to run towards the simple swing bridge that crossed the river. The major, standing on the bonnet of his jeep, saw it too and shouted over to me to intercept the boy. I ran across the compound to the breach in the fence, which Brody's contingent of soldiers was trying to clear by pushing the group of men and women back towards the centre of the square. I tried to squeeze through the fence where the boy had made his escape, but the gap was too narrow. The major had stepped down from the jeep and followed me across the compound, anxious to avoid the prospect of four thousand Cossacks witnessing one of their number, even a child, escape across the river and into the woods in case such an action encouraged a mass break-out from the camp. The boy had reached the little bridge below us and was picking his way across.

'Shoot him.'

I turned round to the major. 'He's a child.'

'The entire fucking camp will make a run for it if he gets away. Shoot him.'

I drew my pistol. 'He's one child. What does one child matter?'

'Captain, if you don't shoot I'll have you arrested for aiding the enemy.'

'He's not the enemy, he's a child.'

'Shoot, damn you.'

I lifted my pistol from its holster. My arm was shaking. The boy had reached the middle of the swaying bridge. I lined him up. I steadied myself. The boy looked round. He saw me. I remembered his name. His name was Leo. He turned forward once more and resumed his shuffle across the bridge that would lead him out into the woods. I could see him in my sight. I could feel the tremor of my breaths make the gun twitch in my hand. I looked at the gun. I lowered it, then dropped it to the ground. I heard the sound of it hitting the earth. A single shot rang out. The ricochet of the pistol shot sounded once against the hills, and then the world fell silent. The boy on the bridge stumbled to one side, swayed, then toppled clumsily into the sweep of the river. I turned round. Brody's arm was still out. He was looking at the spot on the bridge where he had taken aim at the boy.

45

I SIT SHIVERING IN A CHAIR in a corner of the visitors lounge, even though, outside, the day is still warm. There is one other woman sat in the room, waiting, looking away out of the window. She doesn't look round, doesn't notice me, or else she pretends I'm not here. She is preoccupied. I'm only Mouse. My glasses are smeared. My eyes are raw. My hair is damp and matted. I look like a runaway. I am a runaway. I wish I had wishes. I wish the woman wasn't here. I wish I was on my own in the room. I swing my legs to and fro and wait for news of William from one of the nurses, but none comes.

I had enough money in my coat to catch a bus into Bury. I took the Metro across the city. I had my note written out and ready for the inspector.

I think I dropped my ticket. I cannot speak.

I was ready to run if I needed to, but no one asked me for my ticket.

They won't let me go in to see him. William's had a seizure. The paramedics are with him now. Alice told me to wait in here. She's had to go to a different emergency in the other wing. People die here all the time. The other person in the visitors lounge looks out of the window onto the garden, waiting for her own family emergency to unfold. She fiddles with her mobile. She puts it to her ear and waits. It seems as though an answer message kicks in.

'I don't know anything definite yet,' she says quietly into her phone. 'I'll call you back.'

She looks out of the window again.

I take my own phone out. I compose a text to send to 266.

I liked the J. D. Salinger story even though I didn't understand it all. I think my friend might have died.

I press 'send'.

I see it go, picture it travelling out into the world, like a small bird over the roofs of all the houses.

I think of Sadie telling me about the carrier pigeons.

The woman's phone across the room pings with a text of her own. She looks at it and composes her own text in response. She presses 'send'.

My own phone pings.

I look across the room at the woman.

I look down at the text.

I think someone I know is dying, too. I'm glad you liked the Salinger. I think you'll love Franny when you get to know her.

A door slams somewhere down the corridor. I hear a faint shout.

I look over at the woman again.

I type another text. I wonder what will happen next.

Excuse me, I type into the phone, *but do you know William Crosby?*

I press 'send'.

Across the room, the woman's phone pings.

She reads the text. She lifts her head and looks across at me. I feel a little scared, seeing her stare into me like that. I turn away, then steal another glance at her. And slowly, like the blurred image of a camera sharpening its focus, her features form into something recognizable, and I see the shape of William's face in hers.

Her serious expression unfurls into a smile I feel I somehow know.

'I'm Becky,' she says across the room to me. 'I'm William's daughter. I think you've been texting me. I'm here because of you.'

46

My dear girl,

We don't grieve any more for the victims of Ispahan. We don't remember those lost at Nishapur. The destroyed and the dispossessed are like grains of sand, like stars in a sky too vast to comprehend.

I tormented myself for years over what became of you. Simple things are easily enough revealed. I know that the generals were shot in the Lubyanka; that the Cossacks were dispersed to labour camps to dig coal or salt so far out of sight of the world that there were not names on maps, only numbers, for the places they were sent to. I know that seven thousand of them died in the first year alone; that half of them never left the camps. I know that near the barracks at Peggetz a cemetery was built, in which some of the Cossacks who were killed there, and some who committed suicide, are buried. I know that a Russian Orthodox church was built at some point afterwards in Lienz and came to be supervised by an old, one-eyed Cossack, who had survived the deportation.

But the detail is harder. There are things that can't be known.

What happened to you? Are you out there still? Is your mother?

The last time I saw Anna, she was climbing into one of the lorries. She was being helped by the wife of one of the old generals. She would not look back, only forwards into the lorry, towards the journey she was about to make, to become so small a part of a tragedy too huge to contemplate. She would not look back.

Are you out there, still?

47

IT'S JULY. WE'RE IN THE Caffè Nero. I've come from my session with Sadie. Lucas wears a T-shirt and some baggy jeans.

'Your face has changed a bit,' Lucas says. 'And you're definitely taller.'

It seems a ridiculous thing to say. Other people change. I stay the same. I'm Mouse. I don't know what to say to him, whether to tell him he's mistaken, or to say that he's grown even taller, or to thank him. So I shrug noncommittally, a gesture which gets lost inside my coat, which is still too big for me, even if I have grown just a small amount.

'I'm sorry,' I say. I look away from him.

I try to explain about Max but it's not easy.

'I thought you didn't like me any more,' Lucas says.

'It wasn't that.'

'I got angry at those stupid stories you kept telling me.'

'I didn't mean to hurt you.'

'I just wanted to help.'

'I know. I know that. I'm sorry.'

'I know you were just trying to look after your mum.'

'I'm not doing such a good job, am I?'

'Yes you are.'

I tell him about the school I'm going to start in September. I tell him Mum is working part time, that she's started taking a few cases again. I tell him about our new flat in the city that we're leasing until the money from the sale of the house on the avenue comes through and gets split half and half between Mum and my dad.

There's some stuff I don't tell him. I don't tell him that I took the padlock off the outhouse before we left the farmhouse, or that I cut the rope holding the gate shut at the bottom of the field. I don't say that there is a note waiting on the kitchen table for the new tenants telling them that Anthony would make quite a good volunteer to have working in the walled garden. I don't say that the number chalked up on William's kitchen wall when we arrived is the number of his daughter's mobile phone, the one scrawled there by his carer, the one that William tried to ring every day in the month before his final stroke, the number I inputted into my phone but then forgot to alter in order to create a new random number to send my texts to. I don't tell him that I finally got my forgiveness machine to work; that I wrote out some things on pieces of paper torn from my Filofax and fed them in, that I watched them swish through the loop and curves of the pipe, that I saw them sucked into the whirring teeth of the shredder at the other end.

I'm busy thinking about these things that I can't yet tell Lucas. Then I look over at him and notice that he's smiling at me.

'Are you not warm in that coat in here?' he says.

I think about his question. I lean across the table and say, 'At least my jeans aren't hanging down my backside,' in the thin and scratchy voice that I'm still getting used to.

Lucas laughs. Pavel comes over, clearing tables. He gives me a stupid grin like he knows exactly what's going on, which he so doesn't. But when it's time for us to go, I leave a tip in the dish on the counter.

'Dziękujemy!' he says, with a slight bow of his head.

'Proszę', I say, which is Polish for 'You're welcome' and is my one good thing for today.

48

My dear girl,

I want to tell you what it is to be fifty.

For a while, it seemed a forlorn hope that I could make it to twenty-five. But the smell of death has disappeared, and now I find that the years simply will not stop and that no amount of wishing can make it any different.

I have tried to tell you, over the years, about so many things. In return, you can tell me nothing because, for all I know, you do not even know of my existence. Perhaps you do, but are unable to write. This is the finger-hold that I cling to on the ledge when the blackness comes – that you know, or will know one day.

You have reached the age now when you are older than I was when I met your mother, when your people gathered in the valley in Lienz, when each morning the sun shone more piercingly than the day before, when each day seemed so close to heaven.

There was a time when I drove myself crazy reading everything I could about what might have become of you and your people. There was a time when I wanted to feel those things myself. I used to take myself onto the moors for hours, days, telling myself that if this was what you and your mother were experiencing – the cold, the hunger – then I needed to feel them too. It was the only connection I had with you, to feel the same things. But how could they be the same when I could come down off the hills whenever I chose, take a warm bath, use a dry towel, eat a meal, lie in a clean bed? And so I stopped and chose to face away and live a life. Not the one I would have had, but the one that was on offer, a lesser one, but one with its compensations.

And now I find myself at fifty, not so very much changed from the boy who fell in love with your mother, with Anna – my hair a little thinner but the rest of me hardly altered, it seems, after twenty years on my few acres in the hills. I am still a physically strong man. At fifty, my muscles retain the memory of youth. On their good days, I can persuade myself that I am little different to the soldier your mother would recognize. When I am not teaching I can walk contentedly all day across the moors; I can chop wood, plant seeds, mend roofs. Emerging from my bed after a night's sleep is a truer test. Then, I can feel the ache in my hip, the soreness in one knee, the ligaments that will not hold the other knee steady if I rise too quickly from the ground, the bone-deep weariness that descends for perhaps a week once every winter.

I remember myself as a small boy on a beach somewhere, willing the tide to go out. I have a photograph of it somewhere in the house. I look strangely defiant in the picture. I look at my reflection shaving, sometimes, and glimpse him, that boy, or what is left of him. I used to practise shaving secretly by using a toothbrush to scrape my father's lather from my cheeks, so I would be prepared for the adult world. Now, as I straighten my tie in the mirror, I catch sight of my father's ancient face in the creases on my own brow. I wonder sometimes what I would say to him if we met, that pale-faced boy and I, on the beach. I think I might tell him to take his shoes off and paddle in the sea a while.

At fifty it occurs to me that, for the first time in my life, I find I can look forwards and back with equal clarity and equal mystery. I can see how far from the boy I once was I have travelled, and the distance I am from the ageing man I will one day be. How many different people must we be in a life stretching out that far? The old and young me could stand here today almost as strangers, with only the thinnest thread connecting us. We are separated by all those forces that push out of reach the world we wanted, the one we worked for, and, in the process, erode us, wear us down into different creatures.

And what of you, my dear girl? You who are still my little girl with no name, though now you are a woman of twenty-five. I feel I should share with you that my English wife married me with all of her heart and, in return, I gave her perhaps some stony corner of mine. You will have seen too many bad things in your short life for a confession such as this to shock you. My wife and I have a marriage of imagined slights and simmering grievances. Sometimes nothing she can do will allow me to forgive her crassness or the smallness of the provincial world inside her head, not even her eagerness to be excused. The jarring notes of her apologies leave me unreasonably despairing. Sometimes, it's true, I've felt an alignment of mood and circumstance, like the geometry of some rare solar eclipse, that has allowed me to believe I loved her, but more usually our orbits are stubbornly unaligned. It doesn't excuse my occasional straying from the marital bed. My weak man's defence is that there are worse things I have done. Sometimes I tell myself that she sees through my pretence, and therein lies a separate agony. Is what we have, which is so little, better than nothing? Am I an honourable man for staying, or a coward for staying quiet? I tell you, my dear girl, you can find a hiding place, build a hillside fortress, take refuge from the world, but something will eventually seep in. Your weaknesses will find you in the end.

I said there were compensations. Please God, even if we never meet, if your mother chooses never to let you know of my existence, if she has gone by now and you grow old still wondering about me, I only hope that you are blessed with the same compensations. As I type this letter, I can look out through the window of my study and see Rebecca at work in the walled garden I built as a young man twenty years ago, soon after I first arrived here. She is eleven now, tireless and devoted – a small, industrious, magical mouse of a girl, uncompromised as yet, unsullied by the world. I tell myself that she understands me. We talk to each other much of the time without words being exchanged. Each time I glance up from the typewriter, I see her moving lightly about the garden. She is my other girl. She is my hope just as you are. She is the chance I have for restitution.

Yours in love,
William

49

AND AS FOR ME?

My name is Anna de Bruin.

My surname comes from my father's family, from Dutch Huguenots who fled persecution in boats, a surname traced back, my dad says, to 1781, through a line of scoundrels and cheats, angels and saints, all wrestling with life, all bound together in love and struggle and acrimony. Sometimes I picture my dad scouring the past in the same way that he scours the night sky with his telescopes, searching for the ancestors he has developed a passion for tracing, as if to know more of them is to know his own imperfect self a little more each time.

My first name was gifted to me by a thousand years of Cossacks, the last generation of which gathered together in a valley in Austria in 1945, including the Anna from whom my name is drawn, all hoping for a promised land, a happy end to their exodus, their long march, a clean and simple resolution.

My voice was bequeathed to me by William Crosby, at whose funeral, some years ago now, I would have liked to read the epistle, or say a few words about him. Instead, I lay out his life here, dug from crevices and cracks. I once imagined that, when it was done, it would be a polished and spherical thing, a hard mass pressed together and chiselled as if from clean, firm stone. In the end, it sprawls elusively, half-dreamed, and I can scarcely point to the tangle of where it starts and where it ends, where he starts and where the breathing and dreams of those around him, those surrounding him and opposing him, start and end.

And so it ends. They are no more, the girl with no name and the William I came to know, the William whose life for a short while I lived beside on a Pennine hill; the William in whose house I listened to the wind sigh, in whose house generations had listened to the timbers creak like bones; the William in whose shoes I walked, in whose fields I shooed the crows and watched them flap inelegantly into his trees that, before him, were another man's trees.

I carry him with me, as he carried her.

My name is Anna de Bruin, and I have a voice, and it is here.

Author's note

As war ended in Europe in May 1945, around thirty thousand Cossacks found themselves stranded in a valley in southern Austria close to the Italian border. They were less an army than a people in transit – men, women and children, horses and camels, wagons and tents.

Mouse and the Cossacks is a work of fiction. The characters of Anna, Vasilenko and Sukalo are an invention of mine. Other than this, the incidents described in the novel are based on actual events which took place in the Drau valley in Austria between May and June 1945.

I owe a debt of gratitude to a number of historians and their works in my efforts to capture the essence of what took place in southern Austria in the summer of 1945, including Nicholas Bethel's *The Last Secret*, Nikolai Tolstoy's *The Secret Betrayal/Victims of Yalta*, Philip Longworth's *The Cossacks*, and Peter Huxley-Blythe's *The East Came West*.

As Nicholas Bethel observed, it is poignant to note that seven years later, in 1952, the communist side in the Korean War demanded the repatriation of all Chinese and North Korean prisoners as part of ongoing peace talks, irrespective of their wishes and if necessary by force. This demand was rejected outright.